THE VENGEANCE MAN

DAN J. MARLOWE

Black Lizard Books

Berkeley • 1988

ISBN 0-88739-040-4
Library of Congress Catalog Card No. 87-72705

Manufactured in the United States of America

CHAPTER I

THE LOW-LYING, late afternoon, Moline, South Carolina, sun streaming through the windshield nearly blinded me as Wing Darlington swung his fender-dented Galaxie into Shadylawn Terrace. His bronzed, corded forearms cradled the steering wheel. He was talking about our chances of being low bidder on the Edmonds Road job. When I saw that my mud-spattered station wagon was the only car at the curb in front of my house, and that my wife Mona's Pontiac wasn't in the garage, either, I felt a tingle. Maybe today was the day. "Carry me on over to Perry's, Wing," I said, interrupting his disparaging remarks. "I'll walk back."

He jammed his foot down on the accelerator again and the Galaxie leaped ahead past the big house I couldn't afford. Wing drives like he does everything else, fast, hard, and often, because Winfield Adair Darlington is a hard-charging country boy who also manages to look like a movie idol. He's a lean sixfooter with perfect features, perfect teeth, and crisp blond hair that curls even when he's in the water. When he smiles his go-to-hell smile with the white teeth splitting the Spanish-leather hue of his suntan, the women fall down in rows. Although I'm the same mahogany color as Wing, I have more trouble with my women. It might be because my hair is black and I wear it in a flattop. Or because, while I'm just as lean as Wing, I'm two inches taller and twice as wide. Or because I've never been asked to enter a Mr. Apollo contest.

He was still needling me as he pulled up in front of Perry's Liquor Store, a quarter mile from the house. " 'Pears like with your father-in-law's political connections, we should be gettin' a better smell on these county bids, ol' salty dog," he said.

" 'Pears like with your ex-girl friend ownin' a bank an'

5

your ex-best friend a vice-president in it, we shouldn't be so stretched out for financin' "—I gave it back to him pork gravy style. He grinned at me. Wing and I have been partners for four years in the Darlington-Wilson Construction Company. I'm the engineer and he's the superintendent. We're a maverick outfit, specializing in road paving when we can get it, but willing to sink a tooth into anything we get turned loose on. I don't know any two men in the state who work harder, but that isn't what cuts the mustard around Moline, South Carolina. If a man who knew his business were asked to rank the contracting firms in and around the city, the Darlington-Wilson Construction Company wouldn't even make his list. I'd made up my mind a long time ago that I wasn't going to let it stay that way.

"See you in the mornin', hoss," Wing called back cheerfully as he drove off.

I went into the liquor shop. Doug Perry had seen me coming and had a fifth of Jack Daniels sacked up beside the cash register. "Hot one this evenin', Jim," he said as I paid him. He was a round man, with a shiny, sweating, bald head. "Must be rough on a big man like you."

"Not for us local boys," I said, deadpan. "It's only you carpetbaggers from Richmond who mind the heat."

"I've lived in this town twenty years!" Doug began indignantly. Then he laughed as I walked out to the street. "Always kiddin'," he called after me.

I took my time going back to the house. Not a breath of the August air was stirring the drooping leaves of the magnolia tree in the front yard. There was a note from Mona on the kitchen table: "Shopping with Lud. Back by eight." I read it twice. She *could* be shopping with Ludmilla Pierson, her best friend, although on the last two Wednesday afternoons, she hadn't been. I glanced at the kitchen clock. Ten after five. If it was going to happen, this was the time for it to happen. Mona's father, Judge Tom Harrington, the political bête noire of the Darlington-Wilson Construction Company, had gone over to Charleston on Monday for a prostate operation. With the old wolf out of the way, I just might have a chance. If Andy called . . . I crumpled Mona's note and threw it into the garbage bag under the sink.

I ignored the sacked-up Jack Daniels and had a bottle of gin down from a shelf and a tray of ice cubes out of the refrigerator when the telephone rang. I could feel my stomach muscles tightening as I went into the front hall to answer it. "Jim?" It was Andy Martin's slow drawl. "They're in room twenty-four at the Stardust. I'm leavin' this instant to pick up my witnesses an' come by an' get you. You be ready, y'hear?"

"I'll be ready," I said. Then I hung up. Andy Martin was as much as Moline afforded in the way of a private detective, but it seemed that he was enough. It would take him at least fifteen minutes to drive from the Stardust Motel to my place, plus however long it took him to round up his witnesses. I had plenty of time.

I went to the sink and retrieved Mona's crumpled note from the garbage bag and placed it on the table. I removed the Jack Daniels from the sack, split the plastic seal around the cap with a thumbnail, removed the cap, and took a long double swallow. Then I poured half of the fifth down the sink drain, being careful not to splash it, and rinsed the sink out. I left the still-open fifth and the melting ice cubes on the counter. The gin, I returned to the shelf.

I went back to the telephone and dialed the Pierson number. "Jim, Lud," I said when she answered. "Is Mona there?"

"She left just a few minutes ago," my wife's best woman friend answered promptly. As always, when she spoke to me, Ludmilla Pierson's voice took on the bright, hard tinkle of crystal. Lud and Mona had been roommates in college. Ludmilla was the only daughter of the deceased town banker; Mona was the only daughter of Judge Tom Harrington, the wheeler-dealer politico who ran things in the county. Wing, Ludmilla, Mona, and I had been in high school together; we were all within a year either way of thirty. We'd knocked around as a group with some crossover dating. Wing hadn't finished high school, let alone gone to college, but even so, Lud

7

had waited a long time for him to propose to her. When he didn't, she married George Pierson, whom she was now pulling by the ears up through the bank hierarchy. George and Wing had been best friends in school, but Ludmilla skillfully split them up. I'd seen her still looking at Wing occasionally when she thought no one was watching. I didn't think she was in love with him; he was just something she'd wanted and hadn't got yet. I'd never asked Wing how he felt about her.

Mona and I had kicked a few gongs during those years, but eventually we drifted apart. Five years ago it had flared up again unexpectedly, and one weekend, we'd driven down to Georgia and got married. Ludmilla hadn't approved. Judge Tom Harrington—the "Judge" was a courtesy title from a tour on the circuit court years ago—hadn't approved, either. He had bigger game in mind for his only daughter. From bankers and politicians in Moline, I'd had nothing but a hard way to go ever since.

"I believe Mona had another stop or two to make on her way home," Lud was saying.

I'd known she'd lie about it unhesitatingly. I just wanted her to remember my call afterward. "She should be along soon, then," I said before I replaced the receiver.

I went into the living room and opened the safe behind the picture of the four-masted schooner on the north wall. I scooped up an elastic-banded roll of money and closed and locked the steel door again. I replaced the picture and carried the money to the Queen Anne desk that Mona had inherited from her grandmother. I sat down gingerly in the matching chair that had never been constructed to hold my weight, and rapidly made out, in duplicate, a deposit slip for the total of the amounts shown in a rent collection ledger I took from a drawer. Collecting rents was one of my keeping-the-cookies-on-the-table sidelines. I counted out enough bills to make up the required amount, folded and elasticked them into the original deposit slip, and shoved the bundle into my hip pocket. I stuffed the rest of the money into a side pocket.

From another desk drawer, I removed a Smith & Wesson .38 police special, clicked off the safety, thumbed a cartridge up into the empty chamber, slipped the safety back on, and dropped the heavy weapon in my jacket pocket. I left the living room, leaving the rent collection ledger and the duplicate deposit slip on the desk top. Ten minutes after receiving Andy Martin's phone call, I was out in front of the house again, getting into the station wagon.

I drove directly to the Stardust. Mona's Pontiac wasn't there, but Bailey's car was. I parked beside it, got out, and approached the door of number twenty-four. The sun was almost down, but it was still light. The shades were tightly drawn, and I could hear the rasp of the air-conditioning. I bent down to get my left shoulder on a level with the door's lock, and then I rammed against it solidly. A panel of wood splintered noisily, but the lock held. I backed off and hit it again. The lock burst with a whining screech of metal and the door flew inward to hang, sagging, on a broken hinge. I drew the .38 from my jacket pocket, flicked off the safety, and stepped inside.

Every light in the room was on. Whit Bailey, the mayor's son, was on his feet beside the bed, his pretty-boy face blank with shock as he stared incredulously at the .38. With a position disadvantage to overcome, Mona was still rising. Both were needle-naked. Mona came toward me, squarely into the teeth of the Smith & Wesson. That was part of her trouble; she was convinced that all ordinary laws were suspended for Mona Harrington Wilson. I pulled the trigger twice, just as she started to say something. I'll never know what it was. For a fraction of a second I could see the double dimple in her sweaty flesh just below her left breast where the slug caught her; then the dimples exploded outward in a froth of blood. She staggered sideways and slid to the floor in a long diagonal. The only sound she made was a kind of questioning mew. I knew what she meant. This couldn't *possibly* be happening to *her.*

I walked over and looked down at her. Even if I hadn't seen where the bullets stitched her, I'd have known from her eyes that she was gone. I turned

9

and looked for Bailey. He was standing petrified, goggling in horror at Mona's body. He felt rather than saw me turn toward him. Screaming hoarsely, he jumped back onto the bed, face down, his head wrapped in his arms. I stepped up to the side of the bed and put single bullets through both his buttocks, deep. His screaming soared, and he flopped onto his back like a grassed fish. The scream choked off in a gasp as his new position put pressure on his wound; he rolled onto his side. I leaned down over him, reversing the .38 in my hand. I turned him onto his back again, unpeeled his arms from his head, and went to work on his face with the butt of the Smith & Wesson.

I was still busy when the first wave of gabbling fools rushed through the shattered door and grabbed me by the arms. I shook them off, tossed the .38 onto the bed beside the unconscious Bailey, and sat down in the room's only chair.

"Call the police! Call the police!" someone was yelling hysterically.

Eventually someone called the police.

I sat in the chair looking at Mona while I waited for them to get there.

It was just as sticky as I'd known it was going to be.

"Don't turn a wheel 'til Chet gets here," was the first thing I heard from the uniformed police, who were the first to arrive. This was when they found out who was involved. Chet Dorsey was Chief of Detectives and one of Tom Harrington's boys.

When he got there, Dorsey supervised Bailey's removal in an ambulance before turning his attention to me. "Smells like a distillery," he snapped after shoving his red-veined nose into my face. "Take him downtown."

Five plainclothesmen made the trip with me. They were handicapped by the fact that quite a few onlookers had seen me leave the motel intact, and also that with so many of them in the cruiser, they got in each others' way. I knew three of them personally, too, which made them a bit conservative, but I was lucky that it was a short ride. Sometime during the trip, my jacket split right down the back. When we reached the station house, they rushed me into a small room that was bare except for a single chair. And the questioning began.

"How did you find them, Wilson?"

"You planned it all, didn't you?"

"You waited for this chance, didn't you, Wilson?"

"Admit that you planned it. Admit it."

"Will you talk, damn you?"

"You're going to make a statement, Wilson. Make up your mind to it."

I told them nothing. Dorsey was nowhere in evidence. The personnel asking the questions kept changing. They'd cleaned out my pockets at the admitting desk but hadn't booked me. For some reason they'd left me my watch. After four hours of hacking around with nothing out of me, a new team of three men came in. I knew two of them: Zeke Williams from the west side of town, and one of the younger Moody boys. There were five or six boys in the Moody family, look-alikes, all with the same wide-spaced eyes and lantern jaws.

I'd seen the third man around, although he wasn't a local. He was a lean-faced character with a five o'clock shadow. He stood in front of me, smiling, pulling golf gloves on slowly over his hands. Williams looked uncomfortable, and young Moody looked like a man trying to look like a man doing his job. They took hold of my arms and pulled me back in the chair I was sitting in. "You don't need to make a statement, Wilson," the third man said. "All you got to do is sign the one they're puttin' together for you now. Let me know when you're ready."

He had fast, hard hands, and in slow time, he hooked and jabbed me, giving each time to take effect. He worked the belly, the chest, the arms, and occasionally the face. He wasn't punching solidly, but he knew how to snap them off. He took his time, and he kept it up. All my life I'd never doubted my ability to stay the course over any racetrack I was dropped down on, but this boy had me wondering. Although my plan didn't call for it, I was just about to rare back and slam both heels through to his backbone when he stopped and went out, pulling off his gloves.

I spoke for the first time since he'd entered the interrogation room. "I'll talk to Dorsey," I said. "Alone."

They couldn't get him in there fast enough. They took just time enough to clean me up first. I waited 'til the Detective Chief's bulky body was planted right in front of my chair. He was carefully avoiding looking at me. "You know me, Dorsey," I began. He started to pout; it wasn't what he wanted to hear. I continued before he could speak. "Better make the 'accident' fatal because if I make it to the street, I'm holding you responsible. You, personally. Understand? You can't hide from me, Dorsey. Not in this county."

He turned on his heel and walked out; his beefy face was brick-red.

The questioning was renewed, but without the calisthenics. Chet Dorsey knew me all right. Seven-eighths of Albermarle County knew me.

Around three in the morning, they tired of it and slung me into one of Fat Jack Grissom's detention cells. Grissom is the city jailer. The cell furniture consisted of a steel cot without even a blanket on it; but compared to where I'd been, it looked almost attractive. I was soaked with perspiration and would have relished a shower and a change of clothes. Since it wasn't to be, I sat down on the cot, took off my shoes, probed at my ribs gingerly, and tried to organize my thinking.

First, there was the cell.

Ten years ago, in my ridge-running days, I'd buddied around with a boy named Tony Lawton, who surprised me by turning square and joining the police in the next county. For a while he kept coming around on his days off, in uniform, until he realized I didn't feel comfortable around a cop, friend or no friend. He stopped coming finally, but not before he told me stories about police routine and procedure that I've never forgotten.

The only light in the entire cell block was from a head-high, green-shaded light bulb in my cell. No matter where I stood in the cell, its light was in my eyes all the time, while the ceiling was in comparative darkness. I stood up in my socks on the steel cot, put my head above the rim of light, and waited 'til my eyes adjusted to the absence of glare. When they did, I saw it right away. Not the bug itself because I couldn't get high enough, even on the cot, but I could see plainly two thin wires bradded into a supporting joist. They trailed off into the next cell before disappearing into the ceiling.

I climbed down from the cot and stretched out on my back on the cement floor. I chose the corner of the cell that promised the most protection if someone opened the outer door and sprayed a magazine into the steel cot. It wasn't too likely, with Harrington in the hospital and unavailable for decision-making, but it wasn't impossible. Tom Harrington drew a lot of water in Moline, South Carolina, and someone might take a notion to show Tom he was on the team. I'd figured originally that if I stayed alive for eighteen hours after being taken into custody, I had it made, but I still had half of that to go.

The cell was cooler than the night air outside, but the humidity was high. I shifted position from time to time on the damp cement and listened to the jail sounds. Gradually my inner turmoil subsided. I became more conscious of aches and pains, but I surprised myself by dozing off a few times. When I saw daylight at last through the barred window, I had it all figured out: I was in roughly the fourteenth hour of the problem, and I had to think I was on the downhill side of the action.

Nobody came near me 'til Wing showed up at nine o'clock. "Goddam, I jus' now heard it, almos' by accident" —I could hear his furious voice outside the cell block. "Don't you bastards ever *notify* nobody, Grissom?"

"Next of kin," Grissom answered. He sounded nervous. There was a clank of keys, and Wing walked into the cell block. He was looking back over his shoulder at Grissom following him.

"Next of kin!" Wing snorted. He turned his head and saw the locked door of my cell. "Open this heah door, you fatass slug!" he demanded.

"I cain't do it," Grissom whined.

13

Wing's right hand drew back swifter than a striking water moccasin. "Hold it!" I shouted. "One of us in here is enough. At a time, anyway."

The hand dropped reluctantly. "I ought to bust you right down the middle anyway, Grissom, jus' for luck," Wing said softly to the white-faced jailer. "Now haul yourself the hellan'gone out of here."

Grissom needed no second invitation.

I was sure that the only reason Wing had been let inside was so that they could hear what we had to say to each other. He had moved closer and was staring at me through the bars. Before he could say anything, I put my hands to my ears and wiggled my fingers, then pointed to the ceiling. Wing's mouth tightened, and he nodded. There was never anything slow on the uptake about Wing Darlington. His mother had raised no foolish children.

"God almighty dog, Jim, boy," he burst out, his eyes on my face. "You must've—they must've—" He choked it off, swallowed, and started again. "Great smokin' blue hemlock, it scares me to think how close I come to wild-assin' it out to the Sunset Lane job 'thout knowin' a thing about this. If"—his glance flicked ceilingward—"if a friend hadn't called—" his voice died out. "They let you call a lawyer?" he resumed abruptly.

"First time I've heard the word."

"I thought so, after the runaround I got on the phone this mornin'," he said. "So I brought you one. If you can call him a lawyer—he's on'y a kid. Soon's I got the message, I called Vic Cartwright, an' you know what he did? Hung up on me. Our own lawyer, scared green. So were the next two I called. Goddam lawyers in this town don't pull down their pants to crap 'til Tom Harrington"—he paused and spat toward the ceiling—"tells 'em it's time to unbuckle their belts. So I got this boy, if you'll have him. He prob'ly ain't tried but a half dozen cases, an' all of 'em in civil court. He's got it here, though." Wing patted his slim stomach. "That I'll guarantee."

Even a kid lawyer was more lawyer than I'd thought I'd have available. If he wasn't a plant. They could

14

hardly have planted him on Wing, though. "Get him in here and let me talk to him, will you, Wing? Another thing—there'll be some kind of arraignment this morning. Make sure someone from the *Clarion* is there. It might help later on if the public knew I was comparatively healthy to that point. Something else you can do for me. There's a hatchet-faced type on the detective squad, mean-looking but a smiler, a twenty-minute egg. I've seen him around, but I never did know his name. I'd like to."

Wing nodded. "Got you." His grin was wolfish. "An' I'll go get my boy. He's only 'bout yea big, understand, so don't be expectin' Dan'l Webster."

"If he's got his ticket and his nerve, he's good enough for me."

"He's got both," Wing said. "I'll be right back."

It wasn't that easy.

For thirty minutes I could hear scattered phrases of frantic telephoning on the part of Jailer Grissom, interspersed with Wing's hard-voiced sarcastic comments and an occasional softer voice asking Wing to please let him handle it. Finally I heard the clank of the keys again.

"—want you to know I'm only doin' my duty!" Grissom was declaiming passionately as he opened the outside door.

"*Aaahh*, shut your fat, lyin' mouth," Wing said disgustedly.

"Only the lawyer goes into the cell," Grissom said defiantly. "That's orders."

"Orders?" Wing flared, whirling on the balls of his feet. "Whose goddam orders? Grissom, I'll crawl your blubbery—"

"It's okay, Wing," I said. "Keep things afloat, will you?"

"Well—" he said uncertainly. "If you say so." He glared at Grissom, then raised his hand to me in a half-salute and went out.

The lawyer came in and shook hands when Grissom unlocked the cell door. I was probably only five or six years older than he was, but God, he looked young! He was slight in build, but with a good chin on him, and

15

he had sharp blue eyes behind heavy horn-rimmed glasses. "I'm Manley Sloane, Mr. Wilson," he said. "Sorry to make your acquaintance in such circumstances." His handshake was firm.

I had no time to waste. "Who are your folks, Manley?" I asked him.

He was expecting the question. In Albermarle County, where two-thirds of the populace are cousins to each other, it's one of the first asked. "My daddy, Richard Sloane, farms in South Hollow, the other side of Edgemere," he said. "And my uncle, Peter Sloane, sells real estate and is first selectman over in Wiggins."

As I knew just about everyone else in Albermarle County, I knew Dick Sloane and his wife, June, too. Good, solid, reliable country folk. I'd never heard they'd bred any culls. Plus Wing had vouched for the boy. And what choice did I have? "You're my lawyer, Manley."

"Fine," he said briskly. "Let's find out where we stand."

While he was speaking I took him by the arm and led him to the center of the cell. He looked puzzled, but without saying anything, I stooped and took hold of him by the thighs and lifted him straight up in the air—he didn't weigh much more than an average-sized woman—until he was looking right at the bug. He grunted in understanding, his body stiffening in my arms. His voice rose like a bugle. "Jailer! Grissom! Damn your fat soul; I'll have you up on charges for this! You *know* the lawyer-client relationship is a privileged one! GRISSOM! I'll have your—"

He was bellowing right into the bug, guaranteeing a listener a tin ear. I let him down, and he rattled the cell bars, still hollering. He had a lot of noise in him for a little one. Grissom came trotting in, shaking. He'd had a hard morning. "What's—what is it now?" he pleaded. "What's the trouble?"

"Trouble!" Sloane roared. "Any time you plant a listening device in the cell of one of *my* clients—!"

"Oh, that ol' thing." Grissom didn't even look aloft. "That's just in case a drunk tries to hang hisself. It's—

it's not even connected up now, I'm sure. Almost sure."

"Get us out of here," Manley Sloane said grimly.

Grissom hurriedly moved us to another cell, but even after he'd left us again and Sloane and I had carefully inspected the new location without finding anything, we stood in its center and talked in undertones.

"Have you made a statement?" Sloane asked me first.

"No."

He raised an eyebrow. "No? Nothing at all?"

"Nothing."

He shook his head slowly. Like Wing, he'd been looking at my face. "I must be fated for a short life, Mr. Wilson. Our instructor in criminal law was always telling us that some day we'd have a client who hadn't already made a complete confession before we talked to him for the first time, and the day we did, the end of the world was at hand."

"Let me tell you how it happened," I suggested.

I told him, properly expurgated.

He listened until I finished without interrupting. "I don't believe the coroner's jury will even recommend passing it on up to the grand jury," he said then. "Unless"— he frowned. "There's the personalities involved, of course. There'll be pressure." He was silent a moment. "But even if they bind you over, a trial jury will never convict. Not in this county. Not after what you've told me. But I'm positive it will never come to a trial."

That had been my thinking, too, but it was encouraging to hear it from the little man.

We talked a while longer, and then Sloane left. Before he did, he made so much racket about the bugged cell that Grissom didn't put me back into it. When Sloane finally departed after a superfluous admonition to talk to no one but him, I drew a long, long breath. So far, it had gone almost exactly the way I'd hoped. There were still a lot of things that could go wrong, and not much chance to become overconfident, but as I paced the cell and thought it all through again for the hundredth time, I really began to feel that I might beat Tom Harrington's odds board.

17

For some reason I've never understood, coroner's juries in Moline, South Carolina, meet at night; and five days after the fact, I appeared before one. The puffiness had left my face, and my skin is so dark anyway that the remaining marks could hardly be seen. The atmosphere in the small, side courtroom was informal. Sig Jacobus, the coroner, was in his shirt sleeves with a big black cigar in his face, and Manley Sloane was the only man in the room—including the spectators in the back of it— who wore a jacket. I knew every man on the six-man jury—in South Carolina, women aren't allowed on juries —and they all knew me. In Albermarle County, it couldn't have been any different.

Our jurors are supposed to be selected from a full panel, but actually, all Sig does is go out on the sidewalk and tap the first six property owners he finds. If he happens to have told six men to be walking in the square that time of evening, old Sig is going to get the verdict he wants. Two years ago, a friend of Tom Harrington's had been involved in a nasty hit-and-run manslaughter case. Harrington's lawyer, taking over for the friend, and wary of Sig's jurors, had demanded that Sig call a new one from the full panel. He'd made it stick, too, although Sig protested that it was just an additional expense to the county. Everyone knew Sig was afraid of the precedent that might loosen his grip. There'd been a distinct coolness between Sig and Tom Harrington ever since. I was counting on it. Sig didn't have to be for me; I just didn't want him to be against me.

Old Bart Simmons, the straw boss at Crater's Sawmill, was appointed jury foreman. The procedure was just as informal as the atmosphere, and the whole thing went along rattle-de-bang. Bill Craddock, the prosecutor, and Sloane continually interrupted each other via verbal harpoons while Sig Jacobus smoked his cigar, asked an occasional question, and took an occasional note. Craddock did a lot of talking to the jury, a wide smile plastered on his face, but Sloane leaned toward me. "He doesn't like it," he whispered. "He wouldn't be pushing it if someone weren't twisting his arm."

18

Before I could reply, Craddock stopped talking and looked in our direction. Sloane got to his feet and strolled toward the half dozen loosely grouped chairs that held the jury. "Gentlemen," he began easily—the little man's dignity was impressive—"I believe you're aware that most of these hearings are almost a foregone conclusion in their result, with the prosecution presenting just enough evidence to persuade you to hold the defendant for the grand jury, without disclosing in full the evidence it has, and with the defense correspondingly sitting on its hands to avoid tipping off its particular line of defense. Contrary to custom, however, you've just heard the prosecution present a great deal of evidence, adding up to not much of anything, in my opinion, but proof in itself of the prosecution's knowledge of the inherent weakness of its case. In turn, gentlemen, I'm going to make an exception of the defense's standard gambit of silence.

"You're all busy men, and I'm not going to waste your time. I'm not going to parade my client before you for you to see the marks on his face. I'm not even—"

"Exception!" Craddock roared, bouncing to his feet.

"Sit down, Bill," Sig Jacobus said in a bored tone.

Craddock sat, fuming.

"I'm not even going to refer to the listening device placed in his cell so that his conversations, even with his lawyer, could be overheard," Sloane resumed. "I'm just going to stick to the facts. In my summation, I must necessarily touch upon matters distasteful both to the defendant and to myself, matters that the prosecution's mistaken zeal to indict forces us to take up. You have heard the case described as one of deliberate, premeditated murder, gentlemen, but I submit to you that Mr. Craddock's own witnesses have proved it was nothing of the kind.

"Consider: the defendant's business partner has testified that on the evening in question, less than an hour before the tragic event, the defendant was in excellent spirits. You have heard Douglas Perry, proprietor of Perry's Liquor Store, testify to the same effect. Douglas Perry testified also to the defendant's purchase at that time of twenty-five point six ounces of a ninety-proof alcoholic beverage. In testifying to the condition of the Wilson kitchen immediately after the tragic event, the prosecution's own witnesses inescapably support the conclusion that the defendant drank some twelve point eight ounces—half the total content—of that same beverage within moments of receiving Andrew Martin's telephone call."

Snow them with figures they know to be right early in the proceedings, the enthusiastic Sloane had confided to me while Grissom was bringing us across the street to the courthouse, and they'll begin to believe everything you tell them. The little man made his figures sound impressive. I must have drunk a thousand fifths in my lifetime without knowing that one contained 25.6 ounces.

Sloane's voice deepened as his glance roved the chairs. "I have listened along with you, gentlemen, to the prosecution's remarks—surely no more dignified a term can be applied to them—to the effect that in the city of Moline in the county of Albermarle in the sovereign state of South Carolina we no longer operate under what was somewhat grandiloquently referred to as 'the barbaric inheritance of the doctrine of the unwritten law.' You heard me object to the remarks as irrelevant, since they bore on no evidence as introduced. Nevertheless you heard them, and you will weigh them as they deserve to be weighed.

"Mr. Jacobus has informed you that your duty consists in binding the defendant over to the grand jury, or releasing him, as you see fit. I will say in passing that, although to this moment you have heard the prosecution speak solely in terms of an eventual indictment for first-degree murder, if you so desire, Mr. Jacobus will inform you that alternative choices exist in profusion, including second-degree homicide, manslaughter, and aggravated assault."

Sig nodded to the jurors. Sloane sauntered up and down before the chairs, his arms clasped behind his back. "Most important of all, gentlemen, you have heard the action branded as premeditated, the most easily refuted point in the prosecution's entire rambling presentation. Consider again: the defendant returns home and finds a note indicating that his wife has gone shopping with a woman friend. I won't bore you with the details of the difficulty I had in tracing the note to have it introduced in evidence. It had been—ah—mislaid. At almost the same moment that the defendant reads the note, he receives a phone call from a private detective pinpointing the wife's actual location as a motel room liaison with another man, the final deterioration of a domestic situation that had led the defendant to employ the private detective in the first place. And bear in mind, gentlemen, that it was not the first such phone call.

"Unquestionably affected by the rapid assimilation of twelve ounces of the ninety-proof alcoholic beverage readily to hand, the defendant loses his head. Instead of waiting for the private detective and the witnesses as directed, and as planned, he drives himself directly to the specified location. Unfortunately, he has on his person a gun. You have heard the prosecution try to make much of the presence of that gun, and you have heard the simple explanation. The defendant collected rents for a number of landlords, and because it was general knowledge that on certain days he carried large sums of money on his person, on those days he carried a gun. He had a permit for the gun. I repeat: HE HAD A PERMIT FOR IT. And you have heard the prosecution somewhat unwillingly concede that, when apprehended, the defendant had upon his person some three thousand dollars wrapped in a deposit slip of current date, prima facie evidence that the defendant was on his way to the night depository of one of the local banks as usual; and as usual the gun accompanied him."

Sloane lowered his voice, and I could see two of the jurors lean forward to hear better. "As a result of the telephone call, the defendant's mind and emotions became inflamed. He burst in upon the woman who was his wife and the man who was with her. You have heard the ugly details. Surely none of us can presume to know what was in his mind at that moment. Premeditation? Say, rather, the simple explosion of a primitive reaction

21

sparked by a sight never intended for husbandly eyes. It was unfortunate that he had access to a gun at that particular instant, BUT HE WAS ENTITLED TO HAVE IT. There was no premeditation involved. You have, in fact, heard a prosecution witness admit that if premeditation had been involved, both parties could have as easily been killed, instead of the defendant's, in the case of his wife's bed partner, resorting to an outburst of impassioned violence highly indicative of his disturbed mental condition. Premeditation? For the prosecution in such circumstances to even raise the question seems to me a joke, and one in extremely poor taste."

His voice rose again. "In conclusion, gentlemen, I will say to you only that in the light of all the evidence presented here this evening, you cannot in good conscience recommend that this man be held for the grand jury."

He bowed, smiled confidently at the jury, and walked back and sat down beside me.

There was a stir in the back of the room, a rustle and buzz amid the scattered knots of listening people.

The jury retired, and we settled down to wait.

They were back in eighteen minutes. "No finding," Bart Simmons said in his harsh voice when Sig put the question to him. "Unan—unan—" He took a breath and started over again. "All of the same mind."

Bill Craddock glared at Sig Jacobus, who smiled winterly. Manley Sloane and I shook hands. Wing rushed up to me with a jubilant congratulatory handshake, but there weren't too many of them; the long arm of Tom Harrington reached into this room, too, although not as deeply as he might have thought five minutes before. "Taylor," Wing said to me, still pumping my arm.

"Taylor? Taylor what?"

"The name of your hatchet-faced detective. The one you asked me to find out for you. Hawk Taylor."

"Oh. Yes. Fine. Hawk Taylor. Thanks, Wing."

"Nice goin', boy," Wing said to a beaming Manley Sloane.

"I got in a few licks never would have been permitted at a trial," the little man confided. "Sometimes strict legal procedure gets bent all out of shape at these preliminary hearings."

"A beautiful job," Wing said emphatically. "An' he's not goin' to be sorry, is he, Jim?"

"That he's not. In fact—"

"You just clear out a corner of your office for a few filin' cases," Wing continued to Sloane, anticipating me. "You're our lawyer, boy. The files 'll be over soon's I catch up with Vic Cartwright an' cut the ground out from under him."

I was looking around for Grissom. I saw him, finally, standing off to one side. "Am I supposed to go back with you?" I called out to him.

"Don't see why 't should be necessary," he replied with an attempt at a jovial smile. "You can pick up your belongin's at the station house when you're ready. No hard feelin's, Jim?"

I looked right through him. "Good night, Manley," I said. "Good night, Wing. I'm going to walk. I feel like stretching my legs again." Wing grinned sympathetically. "See you tomorrow." I left the hearing room, turned left on the oil-darkened wooden floor of the long corridor, and descended the outside marble stairs to the street.

On the sidewalk, I drew a deep, relishing breath of the night air. I looked up at the stars overhead. For an outdoor man, there are not many places worse than where I'd been the past few days. If necessary, I'd been prepared to sweat it out all the way to the trial, but I'd be lying if I said I enjoyed the prospect. This had been the consideration that had held me back the longest.

My thoughts turned to the house on Shadylawn Terrace, the empty house to which I'd be returning now. Naturally, Mona's image came into focus. What did I feel about her now? That was easy. I felt nothing, one way or the other. I'd been feeling nothing for a long time about Mona. For six months after we were married, she'd stood me off about having children. Then she stopped

23

standing me off, but we didn't have any children. It was three years later before I found out by accident that the "minor" female operation she'd had just after the six-month mark in the marriage had been to make sure she'd have no children. I almost divorced her then, but I was already looking ahead. And in the long run, it turned out to have been only Strike One on the marriage.

Mona? No. Mona had already been gone for a long time.

I set off up the street at a fast walk.

CHAPTER II

I INTENDED to go directly to the station house, pick up my wallet and car keys, and get myself home. Tom Harrington might have lost a battle, but he hadn't lost the war, and if one of his boys could line me up properly in a gunsight, he didn't have to lose it. Until I had an umbrella in place, the area around Moline, South Carolina, was no place for me to be exposing myself.

I changed my mind when I saw a light in the second-floor corner office of the three-story building alongside the jail. I detoured to the building's doorway and climbed worn stair treads to the second floor. I opened a door lettered CARTWRIGHT & MILLER, ATTORNEYS. I hadn't made any noise. "Working late, Veronica?" I asked as I entered.

Veronica Peters, Vic Cartwright's redheaded secretary, looked up from her desk, startled. "Oh!" she exclaimed, half-rising. She glanced quickly at the closed door of the inner office. "He's—Mr. Cartwright isn't in right now!"

I started around her desk. She ran out from behind it and stood between me and the door; her violet-colored eyes were wide. "Don't, Jim!" she pleaded. She was breathing heavily, agitating a considerable bosom. I was familiar with the bosom; I'd been getting to it and adjacent precincts for the past eighteen months.

24

I placed my nose inches from hers. "Get back behind your desk, Veronica," I suggested, "before I feed you your gluteus maximus in one-inch strips."

She tried to stare me down. Failing, her eyes dropped, and she stepped to one side. Her full lower lip was trembling. I advanced to the closed door, opened it, went inside, and closed it again. Vic Cartwright was bent forward over his desk, studying a sheaf of papers. Above his thin, pinched features, his gray hair was straggly. "Yes, Veronica?" he inquired absently. "What —" He turned his head and his eyes came into focus on me. He paled as he stumbled to his feet. "Jim! I'm delighted—that is, I just learned—it's good to know—" His voice ran down.

"Send our files around to Manley Sloane's office the first thing in the morning, Vic," I said. "No excuses or delays. If I should get the notion you were stalling to photostat a few items, you wouldn't enjoy it."

His lean throat worked convulsively. "I know you're upset, Jim, and I don't blame you, but circumstances— isn't there some way—"

"There isn't. When I know who my friends are, Vic, I act accordingly. You get the files over to Sloane."

"Wait, Jim," he called as I started for the outer office. I turned and looked at him. "All right, you're entitled to feel the way you do. I let you down." He passed a shaky hand along his jawline. "I want you to know there was nothing—nothing personal in my refusal to act for you when—when Wing called me." His Adam's apple bobbed again. "There was—there had been a prior call." He cleared his throat heavily. "I imagine I'm not giving you any news when I tell you that Tom Harrington has my balls in his nutcracker, to use the vulgate. And I thought—we all thought—well—" He shrugged. "We were wrong. Although—"

"Although you think all the votes might not be in yet?" I asked when he hesitated. "You still think you might have signed up with the winning team?"

He flushed. "I'm raising a family, Jim. I have—well, problems."

"Let me tell you something, Vic. If you were twenty years younger, your family would have the problems because I'd hospitalize you."

"You—you don't mean that—"

"No?" I stared right at him, and he couldn't meet my eyes. "You get those files over to Sloane's."

Veronica was hovering just outside the outer door when I opened it. She circled me quickly and looked in Vic's door, gave an audible sigh of relief, and closed the door. Finding herself standing right beside me, she retreated to her desk, one hand unconsciously smoothing out her skirt. Veronica is more than a little blocky in the butt, but I happen to like them that way. "I'd never have forgiven you if you'd—if you'd—"

I moved toward her, and she put the desk between us. "If I'd what, Veronica?"

"You know. Attacked him."

I advanced around the desk, and she plunged into her swivel chair like a rabbit into its hole. I put a hand under her chin and tilted her face up. "I'd rather attack you, Veronica. Since I figure this office owes me something. Let's have dinner tomorrow night."

Her strange-colored eyes widened again. "You—how could I—you don't mean—"

"Maybe I don't mean dinner," I agreed. "You're wondering how a girl can afford to be seen with such a notorious specimen of wife-killer?" She blinked. "We can fix that," I continued. "I'll meet you at six-thirty tomorrow evening in the parking lot behind Rowley's. We'll go on from there in my car." Rowley's was a roadhouse two towns away.

She was staring up into my face. "I couldn't, Jim. Just because we've—can't you see that things are different now? That you—that you're different? I can't do it. I'm—"

"Rowley's at six-thirty," I said, and I walked out of the office.

I was positive she'd be there.

I picked up my things at the police station after signing a release—someone had light-fingered forty dollars off my roll, but there's a time and a place to make a stink about that sort of thing, and this wasn't it—found my station wagon on the police lot, where it had been towed down from the Stardust, and drove home. The light was on over the portico, and Frank Garvey, one of Chet Dorsey's men, met me on the front steps and handed me the house keys. He had a two-inch cigar stub in one corner of his mouth and a well-chewed toothpick in the other. "Y'hear tell 'bout the burglary?" he asked me.

"What burglary?"

"Yore burglary. Seems as how someone busted into yore livin' room safe the other night an' like to cleaned it out."

"With the police watching the house?"

He shrugged. "Embarrassin', ain't it?"

He followed me inside. I looked at the battered safe without saying anything. Tom Harrington had been too little and too late with that move. Mona's will and a few other important papers hadn't been in the safe since I'd made up my mind three months ago what I was going to do about her and Whit Bailey. I'd driven over to Palmetto and rented a safe deposit box in the local bank under the name of Joseph Winters. Judge Tom Harrington might have the reputation locally of not having made a mistake since 1908, but he'd made one with me. Still, the attempt on the safe was a good weather prognosticator. Harrington was conceding nothing.

When I turned away from my inspection of the damage, Frank Garvey was eyeing me speculatively. It must have been a surprise to a lot of people that I was still walking around Moline, South Carolina, five days after killing Judge Tom Harrington's only daughter. People are always watching to see if the old lion is losing his teeth. Probably no one in Albermarle County thought seriously at the moment that Harrington was losing his, but—there I was, walking around.

He hadn't had a real chance at me yet, of course, except for the first few hours in custody, and he hadn't been around himself to give a direct order that would have let him capitalize on it, something he was entirely capable of doing, judging from past performances. And underlings don't accept that kind of responsibility. It was what I'd been counting on. Afterward, it was natural for Harrington to let the law do his work for him if it would. Since it hadn't, it was into the trenches in earnest.

I hadn't planned to leave the house again until daylight, but the look of the safe changed my mind. What I needed first and foremost was a life insurance policy. I knew where to get it, and sooner, rather than later, seemed to be the sensible order of the evening. Paying no attention to the sleepy-eyed but observant Garvey, I went back outside to the station wagon and drove to Ludmilla Pierson's house. Garvey's car noodled along half a block behind mine. There was a three-quarter moon in the northeast quadrant of the sky, and I hummed to myself as I drove. With a break here and there, the good citizens of Moline, South Carolina, were due for further surprises, starting with Frank Garvey when he saw into whose driveway I'd pulled the station wagon.

The Pierson housekeeper's face expressed shock when she recognized who was ringing the bell. She left me standing on the outside steps while she went to tell Lud who her caller was. I knew Lud would see me, if only to spit in my face. She swept out to the front door in the dramatic manner she'd had even in high school. She's a tall, cool-looking blonde, and while not quite as regal in appearance as she imagines, she makes an impressive entrance. As usual, she was looking down her patrician nose at me. "You've got a nerve, coming here," she started in on me. "You're not going to get away with what you did, you know." Her voice was calm. "You may have bulled that red-neck jury with your tough-guy image and your unwritten law, but there's an older law: an eye for an eye. You're a dead man, Jim Wilson."

"I came over here to tell you why I'm not, Lud. Can we talk? Privately?"

She hesitated before leading the way inside and turning into a small, poorly lighted sitting room crowded with

28

heavy, old-fashioned furniture. "Be quick about it," she said, facing me again. "I despise the sight of you."

"I'll be quick," I said. Looking at her—she was smooth as cake frosting—I found it hard to believe that since her daddy died Ludmilla had been the brains behind the bank, although she never set foot in it. Her classification of southern lady wasn't supposed to know the meaning of work or the odor of perspiration. "You know I'm Mona's heir?" I went on.

"I know." Her lip curled. "An unfortunate residue of the early days of the marriage. You won't live to enjoy her money."

"You talk a hell of a game, Lud, but your needle's stuck. I'll tell you what I'll do: I'll debate it with you tomorrow morning in the high school auditorium." She sniffed. "No? Then listen for a change, instead of talking. You might learn something. You remember eighteen months ago when it looked as if Tom Harrington might finally have put a foot down wrong before the chief witness in the Crescio case disappeared?"

"I remember," she said, her gray eyes narrowing.

"Twenty-five years ago, he'd have lighted up a fresh cigar and forgotten it, but this time he must have decided he'd come too close to a financial feather-clipping party. He has too much to lose these days, so he began transferring quite a few of his assets to Mona."

"Oh, good God!" Lud exclaimed. She was way ahead of me. "Then you're—"

"When we get out of probate, Lud, I'll be worth more than Tom Harrington."

"Now I *know* you're a dead man," she said flatly.

"Wing Darlington's *my* heir, Lud. You think Harrington's going to feel any better with Wing on his back? Besides, it's not quite the way you see it. When I'm ready, and that will be damn soon, I'm taking over from Harrington, with a little help you're going to give me."

She was staring at me. "Taking—you're insane!"

"So I'm insane. To change the subject just slightly, Lud, didn't it surprise you when the blackmailer stopped coming around for his money a few months back?"

Her lips thinned. "I don't know what you're talking about."

"Have it your way. I just want you to know you've got a built-in interest in keeping me alive now, Lud, because if anything happens to me I've made arrangements to have the film delivered to someone who doesn't like you. For the sake of your own dear, velvety skin, you'd better get the word to Harrington that, dead, I'm going to smell up a few peoples' front porches."

A slim, white hand was at her throat. "Film?"

"Film. Spelled M-O-V-I-E. The movie in which you and Mona share equal billing as a pair of accomplished perverts."

Her face was gray marble. "I'll—" She had to stop and begin again. "I'll buy it from you."

"It's not for sale. Just convince Harrington it's better all around to keep me alive, though, and you're in good shape."

"And how do you think I'm going to convince a vendetta-minded man like Tom Harrington of that?" she cried out passionately.

"Explain to him you've just learned of this movie that would be so damaging to Mona's memory."

"After his forcing you to blacken her name at the hearing, why do you think the idea of the movie would affect him?" she snapped. "I was dead against pushing the hearing, and not only for that reason. I *told* them they couldn't make it stick in this county."

"You preferred to have Harrington hire himself a rifle shot aimed at me from the brush on a side road?"

"Exactly," she said coolly.

"You're lucky you didn't win the argument"—I smiled at her—"because perversion is regarded differently in these parts than good, clean old cuckolding. Harrington's own reputation could be involved, and when he simmers down, he'll realize it. You don't need to say anything to him about your own role in the film, of course. Just tell him I came to you about it because you were Mona's best friend. After the old goat has chewed on

30

it a day or two, you and I will go down to his office and smoke a peace pipe."

"I won't do it!" she blazed. "You're not making *me* a pawn in your harebrained schemes! I refuse absolutely to be seen in public with you, in effect, sponsoring you!"

"Smarten up, Lud. You'll do it or I'll ruin you." I paused for a count of five. "And enjoy myself. You're supposed to have brains. Get it into your head that whenever I say so from now on you'll be seen in public with me, or under me if I take the notion. I'm not playing tiddledywinks with you goddam people. You get on the phone to Harrington and get him straightened out." My voice had started to heat up. I started for the door.

"Wait," she said. I halted. "How did you get—you killed that awful man, didn't you?"

"Killed?" I said. "I just bought the film from him when he came around to blackmail Mona."

She was rallying from the shock I'd given her. "If I couldn't buy it, how do you think you could?" She shook her head decisively. "No. You killed him." She was nibbling at her lower lip. "I want that film."

The imperious note in her voice got to me—Lady Bountiful among the poor. "I wouldn't give it to you even if I didn't need it, Lud. You're the one who took Mona away from me, you and all the rest of the laughing people, laughing at poor ol' stupid Jim Wilson. Snickering up your sleeves for years. You remember the sequence in the movie with you and Mona performing squarely in front of a picture of me, both of you laughing fit to kill? I must have watched it fifty times. Nobody laughs at me, Lud. Nobody." I tried to pull up on the reins as anger surged over me.

"I suppose I'm next on your list, then," she said defiantly.

"I've already told you that I have a better use for you. You're my lily-assed lightning rod."

There was a fifteen second silence. Lud's hands were knitted together in front of her, the knuckles showing white. "You're still angry at Mona, Jim," she said swiftly. It was the first time in ten years she'd used my Christian name without my surname. "The film can't do her any harm now, but think what it could do to me."

It was so exactly the sort of self-centered approach I should have expected from her that I boiled over. "Just what the hell do you think I owe you, Lud? I blame you for the whole rotten mess. You're an out-and-out lesbian, or so close it makes no difference. Was that why, when I had your pants down back in high school, I could never get it in you? I used to think then that you were just a natural-born teaser. How do you keep George in line? D'you make a big sacrifice and lay for him once in a while? Or d'you take care of him some other way? You're no good, Lud, not one damn bit of good. I blame *you* for what happened to Mona."

"I'll kill you myself," she said between her teeth.

"It'll be the most expensive luxury you've permitted yourself in some time if you expect to look the people of this county in the eye again."

Her voice was shaking. "I want that film! That damn man—I was drunk, the only time in my life I was *ever* drunk! I've *got* to have it! I want—"

"You just keep on wanting. And turn Harrington's juice off until I'm ready to take care of him myself."

She was staring at me again, as she had previously. "You planned it all deliberately, didn't you?" Unexpectedly, she burst into a flood of tears. "I don't c-care," she sobbed. "You didn't n-need to *k-kill* her. D'you realize sh-she's *dead,* you big b-beast?"

I couldn't have been more surprised if a fountain had erupted through the cement of the front walk outside. Crocodile tears? Or the real thing? Who the hell ever knew with a woman? I turned to the door again. "Keep it clean in the clinches, Lud, because I'll be watching you."

She was still sniffling as I went out into the front hall. Whatever else I had expected from the interview, the sight of Ludmilla Pierson in tears hadn't been one of them. I was still trying to figure it out on the drive home.

There was a car parked in my driveway. I pulled in behind it and sat looking at it for a minute before I recognized Wing's Galaxie. It made me realize I had to keep the screw down tight on my nerves. Wing climbed out of the car, carrying a bag. "Thought you'd be along soon," he said cheerfully, following me up the front steps. He slid the bag into a corner of the front hall as we·entered it. "Reckon I'll bunk down in your guest room for a few days," he said casually, leading the way into the living room and appropriating my armchair.

"I don't need a bodyguard, Wing."

"The hell you don't, partner."

"I don't want the wrong people thinking I feel I need a bodyguard," I continued patiently. I went over to the liquor cabinet and fixed Wing a drink. As an afterthought I made one for myself.

Wing spoke to my back. "In case you ever get to feelin' you did the wrong thing—"

I didn't turn around. I looked down at the bottles I was returning to the cabinet.

"She made a play for me last year. She didn't want me, but she made the play."

I closed the cabinet door.

"I almost told you because I wasn't the only one. Reckon I was afraid you wouldn't believe me."

I carried him his drink. "I still don't need a bodyguard."

He cocked an eye up at me over his first swallow. "Listen, ol' salty dog, all the goddam heroes—"

"I know where the heroes are."

"You tellin' me you don't want me around, Jim?"

I could hear the hurt in his voice. In the past four years there wasn't much that Wing and I hadn't done together. "You know better than that, Wing. There's nobody I'd rather have around, but not right now. Not until a few things get settled."

"You're makin' it sound like a blood feud," he grumbled, tossing off half his drink. "All the more damn reason I should be here."

"Thanks, but no." I changed the subject. "How are we doing out on Sunset Lane?"

"No worse'n usual. Only a dozer an' a back hoe broke down today. An' I caught ol' Willie totin' water from a salty spring, spite of all I've warned him. Ruined the mornin' batch of ce-ment. Jus' lucky I caught it before we had it down on the road." He briefed me in detail, but his heart obviously wasn't in it. When he finished, the silence stretched out between us.

"I won't be out on the job for a day or two," I said at last.

"Good idea," he said, looking relieved. "Goddam brush grows right down to the roadside all along there. But what difference is a couple days goin' to make?"

"A big difference. I'll have an umbrella up."

He waited, but I didn't elaborate. He finished his drink, changed position uneasily in his chair, and rose restlessly to his feet. "Well, if you're sure——"

"I'm sure. Thanks for the offer, partner."

He shook his head dubiously. On his way to the door he retrieved his bag from the hallway. "Seems like you're playin' a lone hand on this all the way," he said on the steps. His tone was aggrieved.

"It only looks that way right now, Wing," I said, trying to soothe him. "You know I can't give the appearance of hiding from Tom Harrington."

"You're s'posed to sit up for him like a gopher at its hole?"

"I have reason to think there won't be any of that."

"You ain't thinkin' *or* reasonin', boy," he snorted. "With a polecat like Harrington? I know a man's got to play his cards the way they're dealt, but—well, you change your mind, you call me, y'hear? Anytime. Any damn time at all." He went down the walk, grumbling to himself.

I'd intended to go to bed, but I didn't feel sleepy. Might as well sit up a while longer, I decided. I went over to the liquor cabinet and picked up my neglected drink. Through the window, I could see the moon outside. I sat down, drink in hand, and began to think.

Whatever he'd heard about me, he wouldn't be expecting me this soon.

When I made up my mind, I nursed the drink for better than an hour.

It was after midnight when I left the house again.

The station wagon bumped down the rutted road that was no more than two wheel tracks, its headlight bouncing wildly from mucky marshland and swamp greenery. I kept watching for the lightning-blasted pine, and when I saw it, I stopped the car. I got out and went around to the rear of the wagon, lowered the back gate, and slid Hawk Taylor, tightly trussed, out to the end of it. I put a shoulder under him, carried him around to the front, and dropped him in the track in the glare of the headlights. His eyes stared up at me. They didn't look the same as they had the night at the station house.

I went to the back of the wagon again and lifted out a crowbar. Then I walked back to Taylor and broke his shinbones with two swings of the bar, first the right and then the left. To give the devil his due, he didn't make much noise. I cut him out of the rope, and he sprawled there, sweating. His eyes were closed, and his chest was heaving as if he'd run a mile.

I hunkered down in the track beside him and waited until his eyes opened so I would be sure he'd hear me. "You're two miles from the highway," I told him. "If you've got any guts, you'll make it. But take a piece of advice: when you can walk, leave town. If I see you around, the next time I pack you out into the swamp you'll be bait for the land crabs."

I walked away from him. By the time I had the wagon turned around and headed back the way I'd come, Taylor was already over on his belly and crawling toward the highway.

I drove home and went to bed.

The buzzer wakened me.

My first glance was at the alarm clock: three thirty-five. My second was at the indicator on the chair beside my bed. A red "x" glowed silently in the square, showing that someone had just stepped on the metal plate inside the back door. I'd had a problem after the blackmailer had showed up looking for Mona; since I'd built it, the doors of my house had never been locked, and I couldn't start then without having her ask questions I didn't

35

want to answer. The solution had been to get her out of town for a weekend and install the alarm system with its warning box in my first-floor bedroom. Mona's bedroom was on the floor above.

I found an electrician in Greensboro, North Carolina, to do the job, and I'd driven him both ways myself to make sure he didn't do any talking about it. He slid a thin metal plate under the linoleum at the kitchen door in the back hallway, a plate under the rug at the front door, and a strip under the rug in front of each of the downstairs windows. The only problem was in the back hall where we had to take up the old linoleum and replace it with new, but it wasn't too much of a job. Mona was surprised to find new linoleum there upon her return, but it wasn't enough of a deal to cause her to comment much. The electrician also put floodlights in the dining room after I convinced him I was serious about it. From then on, the last thing I did each night was to go into the dining room and remove the heavy folds of Mona's draperies that I kept over the lights in the daytime, then set up the indicator box beside my bed. I kept it in a locked closet, and nothing was activated before I set it up and turned it on. If Mona had been any kind of housekeeper at all, she'd have been almost sure to notice the new arrangement of her draperies; but she never did.

I groped for the .38 under my pillow and eased myself out of bed. To reach the bedroom, the intruder had to come through the dining room, and in doing so, he was making a surprising amount of noise. I waited just outside the dining room door, with my finger on a special switch. When I heard a stumbling step well into the room, I touched the switch. A bank of floodlights turned the room into a goldfish bowl. The slight figure in the room's center yipped aloud and pivoted in surprise. I just did stay off the trigger. The man was Albert Brown, a not-too-bright-in-the-head colored boy who did odd jobs around town. He had a gray blanket on his arm, and his color nearly matched it as he stared at me. "I sure didn' know you was home, Mist' Wilson!" he blurted out at last. His bulging eyes were on the .38.

"What're you doing here this time of night, Albert?" I asked sternly.

He held out the blanket. "Mist' Wheeler done stopped me on Pearl Street jus' now an' took this outn' his car an' ast me to fetch it here an' leave it. Seem like they borreyed it when they was watchin' the house while—while you was away. They want it put back, he say."

It was my blanket, all right. Billy Wheeler was another of Chet Dorsey's men. If I hadn't had the floodlights rigged, or if I'd fired without getting a good look at Albert, another coroner's jury getting a look at me in quick succession might have had an entirely different recommendation to make concerning the killing of a harmless, simple-minded, local colored man. "All right, Albert," I said gruffly, shaken by the close call. "You run along."

I followed him out into the kitchen to the back door and watched him go down the path.

Then I went back to bed, but not to sleep. It hadn't been a bad move on Harrington's part, I thought. Not a bad move at all. Evidently a slug from the brush wasn't the only thing I had to fear from the old wolf.

I'd have to check with Lud and see if she'd given him the word. The smart thing to do might be to go and see him right away, although it was earlier in the game than I'd intended. Waiting on a battle-scarred old coyote like Harrington, though, could turn out to be not quite bright.

I'd see him soon. See him, and begin the tooth-pulling process.

The decision made, I fell asleep again.

CHAPTER III

THE NEXT EVENING, I pulled onto Rowley's semi-deserted parking lot at six twenty-five. At midnight the lot would be jammed. I almost hadn't come. What had seemed like a fine idea the night before, when in juxtaposition to Veronica Peters' lush amplitude, had in bright daylight seemed a much less pressing matter.

A bare arm waved to me from Veronica's blue Dodge, and I walked over to it. The redhead sat in silence as I approached her and opened the door of her car. "We'll come back for your car," I told her.

"Where are we going?" she asked, sliding out from under the wheel and pulling down her rucked-up skirt as she straightened up. I didn't answer her. She led the way over to the station wagon. She was wearing a sleeveless pink dress. Redheads aren't supposed to be able to wear pink, but I couldn't see anything wrong with the color scheme parading across the parking lot in front of me. There was a lot less strain on my eyes than on the back seams of her skirt. I was beginning to look with favor upon the program again.

"I really don't know why I came," she said as I handed her into the wagon. "I couldn't explain it to—to anyone. But here I am." She turned her head to study me, as if expecting to find the answer printed on my forehead.

I didn't say anything. Women are always trying to justify themselves to men. And to themselves. A waste of time and breath. A lot of foofaraw for nothing.

"You—scared me last night," she went on. "And after—after what happened—well, I shouldn't have come. I don't know why I came."

"You came because you like getting shafted, puss."

"What a thing to say!" she said indignantly.

"Well?" I challenged her. "What's wrong with a roll in the hay?"

She pursed her full lips. "With a man who so recently —so recently—" She didn't try to finish it. "Sitting in the car waiting, I couldn't find an excuse for myself, let alone expect anyone else to. But here I am. I'm—"

I tuned her out. Conversation wasn't what I wanted from this one. I boomed the wagon down the road. Three miles from Rowley's, a smart farmer had thrown up half a dozen well-separated three-room cabins in a grove of

38

jackpines. No highway signs advertised the place, but there were never any vacancies anyway. Wing and I split the rent on a cabin, year-round, and the others were similarly spoken for. I'd never brought Veronica out here before. Once in a while I used to come out alone for a weekend's quiet drinking, but usually the atmosphere was communal and hectic. I turned into the unmarked driveway and continued along it to the last cabin. If Wing's Galaxie had been parked in the slot, I'd have swung right around onto the highway again and gone to a motel, since in my present state of ripe odor in the town I could hardly expect Veronica to try to smuggle me into her apartment as before. The stall was empty, though. I parked the wagon, got out and fished for my key.

"My, it's quiet here," Veronica commented. She teetered on her high heels in the pine-needled soft turf, and I took her arm. When I had unlocked the cabin door, I ushered her inside. "Isn't it nice," she exclaimed.

Wing and I had spent a few dollars outfitting the interior. We'd hauled a couple of loads of furniture out from town, including a ton-and-a-half air-conditioner. "You like it cool, honey?" Wing used to say to his little pullets. "You jus' let the ol' Wingman push this heah button down an' in fifteen minutes your maidenhair'll be frosted, sugar. You won't have no complaints about the de-froster, neither."

The place had two bedrooms, a john with a fully tiled shower, and a completely equipped kitchen. Veronica tap-tapped from room to room in her high heels, inspecting everything. I had turned on the air-conditioner and had my shirt off already when she came back into the first bedroom. I took hold of her and turned her around and unbuttoned the three little buttons on the neck of her dress at the back. I looked at my watch, stooped, and took hold of the hem of her skirt; and in fifty seconds I had her shucked out of dress, slip, girdle, and bra without tearing a thing. Wing and I used to have contests for cases of beer.

Out of her clothes, there was a hell of a lot of Veronica.

39

"My God!" she said, kicking off her shoes and sitting down on the edge of the bed in her stockings. "I couldn't have undressed that fast myself."

I stripped and joined her. I tipped her onto her back and filled my hands. Then I flipped her onto her belly and filled them again. My response was automatic. "You really do have a big ass, girl," I told her. "Let's put it to work."

One reason I kept coming back to her when I kept telling myself I really didn't have the time to fool around was that she was good in bed. She enjoyed it, and she worked at it. "Not so—fast!" she protested breathlessly, but she popped her weasel before I did.

"Like to shower?" I asked her after we played the last half of the first inning without changing sides.

"Together?" she said archly.

"Sure."

"Don't get my hair wet," she cautioned as she bent over to remove her stockings. She yelped and bounded eighteen inches into the air when I whacked her.

We didn't get her hair wet.

Any that showed in public, that is.

Back in the bedroom, I looked at my watch. I had a nine o'clock appointment with George Pierson. Veronica came up behind me, put her arms around me, and massaged my stomach with her palms. We gravitated back to the bed. Veronica certainly discarded her inhibitions with her clothes. She instituted a couple of new variations on the theme. I responded in counterpoint. "*Owwww!*" she squealed shrilly, bucking wildly and trying to roll onto her back.

"Hold still and I'll match it for you," I told her, turning her onto her stomach again.

"*Ooooooh!*" she squalled. "Jim!"

"Show those to your girl friends," I suggested, letting her scramble free.

For the next few moments the action was voiceless but not soundless. Where the script called for a grunt, Veronica grunted. She was an earnest laborer in the vineyard. Out of the shower again—singly this time—

I took another look at my watch. "Sorry to break up the party," I said. Obediently she reached for her clothes. I sat on the edge of the bed and watched my teeth marks disappearing into her girdle. "What's new at the office these days?" I asked.

She shrugged into her slip. "Not much, unless you count Mr. Harrington sending Mr. Cartwright over to Spartanburg for a couple of days," she replied muffledly.

It was a good thing she was enveloped in the slip and couldn't see me; I had half-risen from the bed before I thought. The blackmailer had been from Spartanburg. Had Lud known it? It hardly seemed possible. Cartwright wasn't Harrington's lawyer, though. Sounded as if the old buzzard wasn't letting his right hand know what his left was doing.

Her slip in place, Veronica had turned around and was looking at me. "Which will give me some extra time off," she said.

"We'll have to take advantage of it," I said, and I thought even better of it as I heard the sound of my own words. A foot in the enemy camp wasn't a bad idea at all, even if the foot had never worn a shoe. Perhaps especially if it hadn't.

From Veronica's seat in the grandstand—hell, from any woman's—I was now an eligible target, of course, once a few niceties had been complied with. And she had to figure she had the inside track. I wondered how long it would be before she took to hinting about marriage. It would be the end of a beautiful friendship. I wasn't about to marry Veronica—or any other woman, for that matter. I'd been that route and learned the hard way that in the Dollar Sweepstakes single-saddle carried the least weight.

I had Veronica back at the blue Dodge in a hundred and twenty minutes, portal-to-portal time. "It's been great," I said, and I was surprised to find myself speaking the truth. I'd unloaded a whale of a lot of tension on that plump white body, tension that had been building up for some time. Why on earth couldn't it have been like that with Mona? I backed away from the

41

thought. It never had been, even at the beginning. "I'll call you, Veronica." She gave me a big smile, and I watched her drive out of the parking lot.

Since Cartwright was in Harrington's pocket, there was always the chance that she'd been planted on me.

I didn't think so, though. Even at her apartment, we'd always been discreet. Although you never can be sure about a thing like that, I didn't think anyone knew about us. But the idea of her having been planted was something to keep in mind; there was no point in becoming careless now.

I made my nine o'clock appointment with five minutes to spare, but George Pierson didn't. I waited thirty-five minutes before giving it up as a bad job and heading on home.

I began telephoning Ludmilla Pierson the middle of the following afternoon when I hadn't heard from her. The fifth time that the housekeeper told me Mrs. Pierson wasn't in and it wasn't known when she was expected, I piled into the station wagon and drove over there. I could see Lud's car in the garage, which was all I needed to know.

The housekeeper opened the front door and stepped into the entrance, blocking it, when she saw who it was. "Mrs. Pierson is—" she began.

"In," I said, cutting her off. I shouldered her aside, and an indignant gasp pursued me down the hall. I toured the ground floor rooms rapidly, but there was no sign of Lud. With the hard-breathing, matronly housekeeper on my heels, I turned to the ornate stairway leading to the second floor.

"You can't go up there!" the woman exclaimed behind me on the stairs. "I'll call the—you have no business in this house!"

I didn't answer her. I went down the second-floor hallway, opening doors. I found Lud in a bedroom at the end of the hall. She was half-reclining in a lounger with a sheaf of papers on her lap and spectacles perched on the end of her nose. A bulging briefcase was beside her chair.

"I couldn't stop him, Miss Ludmilla!"—the housekeeper's shaken voice came over my shoulder. "He's like a—like a steamroller!"

"It's all right, Margaret," Lud said quietly. She removed the spectacles, folded them, and slipped them into a glasses case. "I'll take care of it."

The housekeeper looked doubtful, but accepted the implied dismissal. "What's with the business-tycoon act?" I asked Lud when the door had closed behind the housekeeper.

"Doing George's homework for him," she said. She methodically stuffed papers into the briefcase. Finished, she leaned back and looked at me. "Don't you think you'd better leave?"

The mention of George had sidetracked me for an instant; I wondered if Lud had had anything to do with George's breaking the appointment last night. I shunted myself back onto the main course. "Did you call Harrington?"

"Yes." She wasn't as much at ease with me as she was trying to pretend; the tip of her tongue emerged and flicked lightly over her lips. She had on no lipstick that I could see.

"Did you tell him I wanted to meet with him?"

"No," she said defiantly.

"Then get on the phone to him, damn it. We'll go down to his office right now."

She flushed and started to say something, then changed her mind. "He's not at his office," she said finally. "He's still at home, recuperating."

"It won't kill him to go down to his office for thirty minutes. Call him and tell him we're on our way down there."

She swung her feet to the floor and sat up straight on the side of the reclining chair. "Jim, why don't we—"

"Call him, Lud."

She flared up like a roman candle. "If you think you can—"

"I *am* pushing you around." I made my voice override hers. "Call him. I haven't got all day."

The telephone was on a marble-topped table beside the bed. She got up slowly and went over to it. I was just a step behind her. She had on a bright print dress, and I could see a faint sheen on her bare shoulders and beads of perspiration on her upper lip. It wasn't that hot. I knew it was grinding her down that she couldn't think her way out of the cat's cradle I'd landed her in. She was so used to being in control of a situation that with someone else's foot on the horsepower she didn't know up from sideways. "Hold the phone so I can hear him, too," I told her as she dialed.

She didn't look at me. "This is Lud, Tom," she said swiftly into the phone. She sounded anxious to get it over with. "Jim Wilson's here and he wants to meet you down at your office right away."

She held the phone away from her ear, and I could hear Harrington's cracked voice plainly. "Pushy bastard, isn't he?" he said drily.

"I really think perhaps you ought to do it," Lud said. "We could come right down."

"*We* could come right down?" Harrington repeated, emphasizing the pronoun. "For the record, Ludmilla, whose side are you on?"

"You know whose side I'm on!" she retorted angrily.

"Do I?" There was an audible grunt. "I wonder. You're pushin' me hard on this, seems as though."

"You know how I feel—felt about Mona! I'm just trying to do what's—"

"No sense in our fussin' at each other," he interrupted. "Could be just what Wilson wants. I wasn't goin' down to the office today, but I reckon I can manage it. These damn doctors an' their carvin' on a man—" He stopped. "Half an hour all right?"

"Fine. We'll be there." She replaced the receiver, stood with her back to me for an instant, and stared across the room at the far wall. Then she walked to the door, still without looking at me.

I followed her, feeling the same familiar upsurge of

44

adrenalin I experienced when the bouncing dice rolled down the table top.

Soon I'd know whether I actually had Judge Tom Harrington where I wanted him. I was almost sure that I did, but with an old gray wolf like Harrington, how could I be positive?

Out on the front walk, Lud headed for my station wagon, which was parked in the driveway. "We'll take your car," I said.

She was already stooping to slide into the passenger's side of the station wagon's front seat. Her dress and slip were so thin I could see plainly the outline of her pants on the round bulge of her fanny. She straightened up slowly. "You and your goddammed pound of flesh," she said bitterly when my meaning became clear to her. In my car, there just possibly might be an acceptable explanation for her being with me. In hers, there was no question that she was with me all the way.

We walked to the garage and her car, and she started to head for the driver's side. "I'll drive," I told her. She started to protest, but thought better of it. I backed her car down the driveway, around my station wagon, and out onto the street. I was still thinking about Lud's underwear. It was hard to believe that years ago I'd sweet-talked her out of it, even though nothing had come of it. What had it been like? I couldn't remember. Whatever the sensation had been, it had long since blended with a thousand others.

We headed downtown. She sat erectly beside me, her hands tightly folded over the handbag in her lap. In the square, I parked across the street from the bank. Harrington had his suite of offices above it. "On a day as hot as this, you can certainly park closer," Lud said irritably. She turned suddenly to glare at me. "If you think you're going to parade me around the square like a—like a Roman triumph—!"

"Glad to see you're up on your history, Mrs. Pierson. Prepare to parade."

"I won't do it!" she stormed. Her gray eyes were blazing. "I won't go with you!"

"You're not calling this square dance, Lud. If I have to, I'll carry you. Or if you think your hole card's better than mine, call my hand." There was an electric silence. "Now get the hell out of the car."

She did so, and she was an actress. Before she hit the sidewalk, her thin-lipped mask of anger had changed to her usual smooth-faced, patrician hauteur. Side by side, we marched around two sides of the square to Harrington's office, and to look at her you'd think she'd been doing it every day of her life.

I could picture the rush to the front windows of the shops we passed.

"Isn't that—?"

"What in the world?"

"Why, I thought—"

"Ludmilla Pierson and Jim Wilson, of all people! What do you suppose—"

In Moline, South Carolina, it counts more than in most places whom you walk out in public with.

I knew that Lud could see the picture, too, but her veneer never cracked. We entered the door to the right of the bank entrance and climbed narrow stairs to the second floor. She was two steps ahead of me, and I was again able to observe at close range the play of sleek hips and long legs beneath her skirt. She didn't appear to have gained an ounce since high school. She led the way down the second floor corridor and opened a door with Harrington's name lettered on it.

There were three desks in the first office, two of them empty. Judge Tom Harrington sat at the third. He was a big-framed man, but he looked shrunken, somehow. His hair had been white ever since I could remember, but it had been cut recently by an inexpert barber, probably while he was in the hospital, and the flowing mane that had usually lent him dignity looked like chopped cotton. His face was deeply lined, more so than I remembered it, and his prow of a nose subordinated the rest of his seemingly diminished features. His eyes had a yellowish tinge. I realized that Lud was staring at him, too. Tom Harrington looked old.

"Pardon my not risin', Ludmilla," he said. "These damn doctors an' their whittlin'—" he didn't finish it, and he didn't look in my direction. Even his voice was different. The familiar resonance was missing.

"You'd like to get this over quickly," Lud said. It was a statement, rather than a question. She remained standing.

"Reckon I would," Harrington agreed. One hand rubbed the back of his neck slowly. The yellow-tinged eyes still hadn't come to rest on my face. "No doubt about this heah movie, Ludmilla?"

"None, Tom."

"An' he can do what he threatens?"

"I've seen the—the evidence. He can do it. Dead or alive."

Harrington's expression didn't change. "What's his proposition?"

I opened my mouth for the first time since leaving the sidewalk below. "I'll make my own proposition, Harrington."

The yellow-flecked eyes hit me a glancing blow before returning to Lud. "Reckon you'd best step into the other office for a minute," he said to her, and he waited for the door to close behind her. "Well, Wilson?"

"I want the Edmonds Road job. For a starter."

"You've got it."

It took me by surprise. "I'm talking about the whole contract: grading, drainage, culverts, bituminous paving—"

"I said you've got it."

"Well—" I said uncertainly. The old goat had certainly taken the wind out of my sails. "Then I guess I'll just walk across the street to the *Clarion* office and give them the item." I couldn't resist trying to harpoon him. "Should I tell them we weren't the low bidder?"

For an instant, the glare was back in the tawny eyes. "They know it!" he snapped. The glare subsided. "Tell them anything you damn please, except about one thing," he continued wearily. He appeared to be turning something over in his mind. "I could be a loser all the way around in this jackpot, Wilson. Suppose Whit Bailey's friends get to you?"

"I don't happen to think Bailey's got that kind of friends. If he should, though, don't you think you ought to convince them you have priority?"

He growled something deep in his throat. "If I was—"

"Yes, I know. If you were twenty years younger, you'd exercise the priority."

"If I was a year younger, damn you!" He subsided again, staring down at his desk top.

"We'll have more to talk about later," I said. He didn't answer me. I went over and knocked on the door of the inner office. "We're leaving now," I said to Lud when she came in.

She looked at Harrington for confirmation. "Pardon my not risin', Ludmilla," he said.

At this left-handed corroboration, she preceded me through the outer door. She couldn't wait to get downstairs to the street to find out what happened; she stopped in the middle of the stairs. "Well?" she demanded.

"Wing and I get the Edmonds Road job."

She cocked an eyebrow. "Just like that?"

"Just like that. For openers."

She didn't appear to hear the needle I intended her to get. "He's an old man," she said. There was a wondering note in her voice. "An *old* man." Her eyes focused on me again. "What's the rest of your bargain? Me staked out naked over an anthill?"

"Too good for you, Lud."

She smiled. "Do I have to drive you back to the house?"

"You run along," I decided. "I've got a little business downtown. I'll catch a ride out later and pick up the wagon."

We descended the rest of the stairs, and out on the sidewalk she walked away from me without a backward glance. I watched her go, then glanced around the square. Nothing was moving; people were standing. Standing and watching. I headed diagonally across the street to the *Clarion* office. They wouldn't be surprised at my news item. Tom Harrington had been top dog in the county for a long time, and he worked hand-in-glove with the city's politicians, the people who mattered. And he had pipelines into the important state offices. The *Clarion* people might be puzzled over the reason for Harrington's giving me the job, but not at his ability to do so.

Reb Dunleavy, who had some kind of job in the mayor's office, came hustling out of Abbott's Drug Store and angled to meet me. His jackal face was alive with curiosity. "You walkin', Jim?" he asked eagerly. "Give you a lift somewheres?"

I started to refuse, then changed my mind. Let the word get back where it would do the most good. "Give me five minutes with Roy in the *Clarion* office and you can run me a couple miles out to my car, Reb."

"Sure, Jim. Sure. I'm parked in front of the bank."

Twenty minutes later I was climbing into the station wagon again, after watching Dunleavy's beady little eyes widen when he recognized where it was parked. When Reb rushed back to town and checked on the item in the *Clarion,* and with his other news, he was going to make the *Clarion*'s next edition superfluous by the time he finished broadcasting.

I started back to my house to get my boots before driving out to Sunset Lane to tell Wing about the Edmonds Road job. On the way, I thought about Tom Harrington. The whole affair had gone so easily that there hadn't been nearly the pleasure in it that I'd anticipated. Was there a warning in that? Had Harrington given in too easily? A factor I hadn't considered previously was slowly coming to the surface as one of prime importance: it would be twelve to fifteen months before Mona's estate was settled, twelve to fifteen months before I swung any kind of financial leverage against Tom Harrington. Could he be thinking in terms of sabotage on current jobs that could break me before I got my hands on Mona's—and his—money?

I was going to have to tell Wing to be careful.

There was a black sedan parked in front of my house,

and a man got out of it as I drove up. He was tall, rawboned, and young-looking. He had large ears and a high-cheekboned face whose expression was solemn. For an instant I couldn't place him, and then I did. He was the Moody boy—I couldn't call his first name—who'd held my arms the night Hawk Taylor worked me over at the station house.

He shambled over to the station wagon and leaned in the front window. "Reckoned you'd be lookin' for me," he said stiffly. "Thought I'd save you the trouble."

He'd heard what had happened to Taylor. This was a country boy, right out of the clay hill canebrakes, and the worst thing I could do would be to ha-ha him that he'd just been doing his job and Taylor was the only one I was interested in—which was true. If this type got to brooding afterward and decided I was soft-soaping him against the day I toted him out into the swamp, too, he'd be likely to mount a scope on his deer rifle and do a little stalking of his own.

"Let's go around to the side yard," I suggested.

"Fine," he said. He looked relieved.

We walked around the house to the twenty-by-thirty Anchor-fenced enclosure, unbuttoning as we went. Mona used to keep her dog in the side yard before she got rid of it because the dog paid more attention to me. Moody and I stripped to the waist. On the street he'd looked skinny, but squaring off, I noticed he had long arms and a slab-sided pair of shoulders. In the first thirty seconds, he rattled my teeth three times with punches that seemed to come out of nowhere. It dawned on me then that he was a southpaw and I was circling right into him. I reversed and went the other way, then found I still couldn't get past his right jab. He ticked me off with it steadily until I bulled inside and whaled him with both hands to the belly. It dropped his guard, and I decked him with a chopping right.

He bounced right up again and charged me. We ricocheted off the fence a couple of times, and I could feel skin staying with the fence. After his quick round trip to the turf, Moody wouldn't back up and he wouldn't cover up. He just planted himself, leaned in, and traded punches. He had knotty, plowboy knuckles that cut when they landed. Once I had his style figured, he landed only one to my three, but he threw them steadily from out in left field. He was a willing workman.

It took me another three or four minutes to time his left hand and drop my right over it consistently. Each time I landed after that he went down, and he kept getting up more slowly, but he kept getting up. He was leaking blood from half a dozen gashes, but he kept trying doggedly to land that left hand again in a meaningful way. I feinted him once, then twice. When he reacted, off-balance, I nailed him a lick that sent him staggering backward into the fence. As he reeled forward again, I caught him with a right that picked him up and turned him around. He landed flat on his belly.

I thought that was it, but his knees scrabbled busily, as he tried to get himself started upright again. This kid was really something. I knelt down beside him, then sat on his head. He kicked steadily for a minute, trying to dislodge me, and then ran out of steam. I waited another minute to be sure he'd petered out before I got up. It took Moody a while to stumble to his feet. His arms dangled straight down at his sides, and his tongue licked at a trickle of blood at a corner of his mouth. He kept shaking his head. " 'Fore—God, Wilson, you hit—a mean lick," he panted. He was looking over my shoulder. When I turned to see why, people were lined up two deep against the side fence. No one said anything, and no one had come into the yard to break it up. In Albermarle County it isn't done.

I turned back to Moody. "Let's go inside and clean up."

He nodded, and we picked up our clothes and walked to the gate. My legs felt like lead. The side yard turf was badly torn up. It looked as if a drunken elephant had been taking dancing lessons. Inside, I showed Moody the downstairs bathroom. "Take your time," I told him.

He nodded again. I didn't feel up to any five-minute speeches myself.

I went upstairs to the big bathroom and took inventory. I had a cut over my left brow, a swollen nose, a puffed lip, and purpling bruises on the ribs on my right side. Plus I'd scraped a yard of skin from my back onto the fence. I washed up and took care of the oozes with a styptic pencil. Downstairs again, I went to the liquor cabinet, and when Moody came out of the bathroom dabbing at his face with a wet towel, I handed him the styptic pencil and a three-ounce jigger of bourbon. He tossed the jigger's contents back in a swallow, then stood as if he was listening to something. In forty-five seconds he was green. He dashed back into the bathroom, and he was really racked. He didn't know it, but the bourbon-induced nausea was a part of his licking.

I sipped my own drink slowly, letting it trickle down to my still-churning stomach. It was another five minutes before Moody emerged again, very pale. He'd made good use of the styptic pencil. He had only one slash—high on a prominent cheekbone—that was still bleeding. He also had some lumps that would get lumpier.

"I reckon that was a real kid trick, tossin' that bourbon down," he said, getting into his shirt. If his arms felt like mine, I could sympathize with his grimaces. Our breathing was almost back to normal, though. When he had his jacket on, I put on my shirt and walked out front with him to his car. He looked almost cheerful as he got behind the wheel. He squinted up at me from one half-closed eye. "Good day to you, Wilson," he said. Then he drove off.

It made me wonder what it felt like to be that young again and without a worry in the world. Moody had taken his licking and had lost no face. Around Albermarle County there's nothing more important. Tonight he could walk down Beauregard Street and, in response to joshing queries about his appearance, say easily: "Oh, I drove over to see Jim Wilson this afternoon." Nobody would ask any foolish questions. And if his friends expressed the hope that he had done all right, he could say just as casually: "I reckon he messed up a time or two."

It seemed a long time back to the days when I'd been like that.

With no further need to act like an iron man, I went back upstairs and stripped. I stood under the shower's hot water for twenty minutes, soaking out the major aches. Dressed again except for shoes, I went down to the back hall and routed out my cement-encrusted snake boots. After I had pulled them on, I set out for Sunset Lane and Wing Darlington.

CHAPTER IV

AT MY UNCLE'S place on the edge of town, the barn stood four times as high as the house that had been home to me from the time I was five until I was thirteen. The front parlor had a fireplace twelve feet wide; there were fourteen-foot ceilings in all the rooms, and sixteen-inch oak planks for flooring. People restoring houses would pay upward of ten dollars a board for that flooring today. From the weathercock on its roof to the washtubs out in front, the barn, which was the largest in the neighborhood, received a fresh coat of paint every third year. The house, a shabby, peeling gray-white, was never painted in my time there.

My father died when I was four, and my mother ran off with a traveling man. Or so my uncle told me; I was twenty before I learned she'd married a farm machinery salesman and they'd been killed on their honeymoon when he drove his car into the side of a freight train during a heavy fog. The same party who told me that also mentioned that my uncle had courted my mother for six months before she married the salesman. After the things he'd had me thinking about her, it was a good thing for him he wasn't available to me the day I found it out.

He was my father's half-brother, actually, and a slob.

He had to depend on good hired help to keep the farm going. He and my father had never got along, although I didn't find that out until years later, either. My uncle was a God-fearing man; I heard him say so often enough. He had other favorite sayings. "Preventative medicine," he used to say, snapping his galluses over his pot belly— I've never liked fat men since—and rolling his eyes toward the dog whip on its handy nail in the kitchen. "Preventative medicine. Catch 'em young an' train 'em right. That's the ticket, ain't that kee-rect, Lucy? Ho-ho-ho."

Lucy, his wife, was a wraith of a woman. When two minutes away from her, I couldn't remember her features. She would smile timidly at each such sally of her husband and say nothing. At thirteen, I was six feet tall, but I weighed only a hundred and fifteen pounds, and in my losing jousts with my uncle's authority, I learned that he could take off a right smart bit of skin with his damned dog whip. Since even then I had what could be called an independent nature, the dog whip and I were no strangers to each other.

Not that I felt particularly abused. I knew plenty of kids who had it tougher than I did, and from their own folks. My trouble was that I never learned to keep my mouth shut. Measured against the output of the hired hands on the place, my work was a man's work, even though I was only thirteen. I knew better, since my uncle was tighter than a tractor tire to the rim of its wheel, but out in the barn one day, I told him I'd appreciate a few coins to jingle together in my pocket at the four-corner store come Saturday evening. He turned scarlet. "Just like your Jezebel mother!" he trumpeted, grabbing me and snaking from his pants the belt that always reinforced his galluses. "I'll teach you to want to hang around with other no-goods like yourself, sniggering over Satan only knows what!"

I was afraid of him, but that time I fought him. I think it surprised him that he had so much trouble. When it was over, he stood there panting, glaring down at me on the rough barn flooring between his feet. "Reckon—

you need—t' be shown—a little oftener—who's boss—around here!" he said, wheezing. "Now go tend t' the cows—like y' should've been doin'—in the first place!"

I tended to the cows, and sometime during the process, I decided I wasn't having any more of that. For a week I thought of elaborate schemes, then on impulse acted upon a simple one. I came in from the barn one night with a half a dozen two-foot lengths of baling wire under my shirt. I carried them up to my attic room. My uncle's house was an early-to-bed house, and by ten o'clock it was silent. I made a bundle of my things, then sat by the window so I wouldn't fall asleep. When the grandfather clock in the front parlor chimed midnight, I tiptoed downstairs to the kitchen and acquired the dog whip and a chunk of cordwood from the woodbox. With the baling wire in my hip pocket, I walked boldly into the bedroom of my uncle and aunt.

I'd counted on the fact that he was a heavy sleeper, and he never moved; but my aunt raised her head. "Get out of bed," I whispered to her between his heavy snores. I thought she might scream, but I didn't care. That's why I had the cordwood chunk—for him, not for her. She slipped quietly from the bed, though. I placed my chunk nearby, in case I needed it, then reached for my baling wire. I had my uncle tangled up in the sheet and his forearms wire-wrapped together before he began to come to at all. It took me longer to wire his kicking feet.

I'd been watching my aunt from the corner of my eye, but she had seated herself in the room's only chair. I picked up the dog whip and worked the sheet over from end to end. The sounds that came from beneath it only stimulated me to greater effort. During the whole performance, my aunt never said a word or made a move. I dropped the whip finally, went back to my room to pick up my bundle, and left the house.

I didn't stop walking until I reached the county line; and I slept the next day in a ditch under a cottonwood tree. The second night, I walked across another county and slept out in a cornfield. The third morning, I hired out to a farmer. I told him I was sixteen. I wasn't too much concerned that anybody would come after me and try to bring me back. Anybody official, that is. In Albermarle County, no one was going to interfere with my uncle's dog whip, but no one was going to interfere with my getting out from under it, either.

The second week I was with the farmer, I was bulling a gang plow behind a span of three horses in a field at the edge of the county road. An Albermarle County cruiser drifted by and Deputy Jed Matthews looked me squarely in the eye and then kept on going down the road without a sign of recognition. Years later he told me that after I'd disappeared and they'd seen the shape I'd left my uncle in, there'd been some concern that he might have buried me out on the back forty. When they found out he hadn't, official interest lapsed. No one ever told my uncle where to find me.

I stayed with the farmer for two years before moving back to Albermarle County. I got a room in Moline and a job in the jute mill unloading hundred-pound sacks from freight cars. I'd grown another two inches and put on fifty hard pounds. After a couple of months at the mill, Jed Matthews came wandering into my freight car one day, mumbling that I had to go back to school. I wouldn't have paid any attention to him, but he went to my boss, Rafe Larkin, too. Fortunately, Rafe liked my work well enough by that time to work out a deal. I worked two shifts at the mill, from four to seven in the morning and from four to nine in the evening and in between I went to high school. At first I had trouble picking up in school after a two-year lapse, but I finally caught on to it again.

My algebra teacher was Miss Eleanor Townsend, a middle-aged old maid with a spirit to match her pepper-and-salt hair. She kept telling me I should go on to college, and I kept saying 'Yes,' but I paid no attention. Then I heard she'd tackled my uncle about it on the street one day—he and I didn't speak the few times we met—and he'd said for the world to hear that I didn't have brains enough to pound sand in a hole properly, and he wasn't about to waste money sending me to college, even if part of the farm *was* to be my inheritance at twenty-one. That was the first I'd heard of it.

So naturally I went to college to spite him. Rafe Larkin got me a job in a cotton mill in Charleston, and that carried the load. I'd always liked figures, so I went the engineering route. Summer jobs were easier to get with that background, too, when the mill slacked in hot weather. I was no ball of fire in the classroom, but I burned enough midnight oil to finish in the top third of the class.

Even with my job at the mill, I didn't have money for weekends at home, and not much to go home to, anyway, but my third year at school, I met a good-looking girl who didn't run from me. We had a few dates, and kidlike, I had to show her off. I borrowed a car and drove her to Moline and paraded her around town. The Larkins put her up.

That should have been all there was to it, except that I was me. In one of our walking tours of the town, the girl and I passed the Salisbury Tavern with its usual quota of loungers out front. There was a chorus of whistles, and a heavy voice said distinctly: "Lookit the ass on *that!*" I turned to see who'd said it. That was Mistake Number One—and the only one I really needed to make because the speaker was Luke Johnson, the bully boy of the county. If I ignored the remark after identifying the source, I was branded, and if I didn't, I was guaranteed a great deal more than I could handle.

The girl's hand had tightened on my arm as she tried to walk me past the Salisbury. I shook her hand off and walked over to Johnson, a hulking, black-browed giant with shoulders like a mule's hindquarters. "Maybe you'd like to apologize for what you just said?" I asked him. I was so mad—and so scared—my voice cracked in a falsetto. Johnson laughed, then slapped my face with a contemptuous backhander I didn't even see coming. Furious at myself, I nailed him solidly with my best shot. It moved his head back maybe six inches. He grunted and went to work on me in earnest.

57

For years afterward, people told me solemnly how they'd kept count of the number of times I got up from the ground. Depending on the teller, it varied from thirteen to twenty-one. Toward the end, Johnson's voice changed from a snarl to a plea. "Stay down, you sonofabitch! Stay down!" he kept saying. He was still almost unmarked when he turned abruptly and walked up the street.

I rocked back and forth on my heels, sick and dizzy, trying to remain upright. The girl had disappeared, as any sensible girl would have done. I took an uncertain step, and then another, found I could walk, and wobbled through the Salisbury's swinging doors. The crowd followed me inside, no one saying anything. I hooked my elbows over the top of the bar, trying to look casual and not as though the bar was holding me up. "Whiskey," I said to Al Gershon, the bartender. I'd never had more than a beer in my life, but I tossed the shot of bourbon down the way I'd seen others do. I barely made it into the men's room before spraying it off two walls. When I could breathe again, I mopped the blood off my face with my handkerchief, left the Salisbury without speaking to anyone, and took the back streets to the Larkin house.

The girl had returned almost in hysterics, and Rafe, that patient man, had dispatched his wife to drive her back to school. Rafe patched me up himself, and after a night's sleep, I felt almost human again. Before Rafe would let me drive myself back to school, though, I was two days overdue.

I never saw the girl again, but I never again had trouble in Moline like the Johnson trouble, either.

Out on Sunset Lane, the scattered backhoes, graders, and bulldozers were sputtering, fuming, and smoking. I found Wing holding up a line of cement trucks, their huge drums revolving, while he tested a sample of the cement poured from a drum. He used a hollow steel cone, twelve inches high, eight inches in diameter at the base and four at the top. He poured cement into it, tamped it down vigorously, and repeated the process several times. When the cone was packed solid, he lifted it up by projections on its base and watched the wet cement settle. A two-inch slump was permissible; anything more meant an inferior mix. The county inspector performed the same test at our batching plant before sending the trucks out, but we usually checked it again on the job site, too.

Wing waved the line of trucks ahead to the paver with its maw waiting to receive the trucks' cement, tossed the cone aside, then turned and saw me. His eyebrows lifted comically. "What'n'ell happened to your face?" he wanted to know.

"Young Moody came by to see me," I explained. "He was one of the ones at the station house that night."

"*Aaahh,*" Wing said softly. He had never asked me about Taylor. He was wearing nothing but boots and cement-stiff work pants, and he hadn't shaved that morning. One side of his beard stubble was crusted with dried concrete. "Thought you were stayin' the hell away from the job," he added as an afterthought.

"My umbrella's up."

"You hope." His glance went up and down the raw gash of the gouged-out road. Thick brush grew down close to its edges on both sides. "Makes no sense, your comin' out here, Jim."

"I tell you the umbrella's up, Wing. But let me tell you something really important: we've got the Edmonds Road job."

"Who says?" he asked instantly.

"Tom Harrington."

"That's—great," he said slowly. Then he was silent.

I couldn't understand it. "That's all you've got to say? I thought you'd be turning handsprings in the newest-laid concrete segment. You know what it means to us."

"Sure, I know." White teeth gleamed in his beard-stubbled face, but his usual cheerful grin was rueful. "I just wish I felt I'd a little somethin' to do with our gettin' the job."

It was the last reaction in the world that I'd expected. "Don't be a jackass, Wing. What difference does it make who got it? Who landed the Pulsifer job? I didn't. I didn't have a single—"

"The Pulsifer job was mighty small potatoes an' not very many to the hill, compared to this'n."

"What difference does it make?" I repeated. "For once we're standing out in a rain of soup with a spoon instead of a fork."

Wing was looking thoughtful. "How'd you squeeze the old bastard, Jim?"

I'd already decided how to answer this question I had known was bound to come up. "I'm Mona's heir, you know."

"So? Mona didn't have—" He stopped. "You tellin' me she left you some real money?"

"Harrington had put a lot of his own money into her name recently. Ironic, isn't it? He's got to be nice to me now."

Wing stood with his head to one side as if testing the sound of my words. "It don't sound like him," he said. "He should be fixin' to slab you up in one of these segments an' leave you as a permanent part of this heah Sunset Lane Extension."

"I told him that you're my heir, Wing," I said patiently. "That's the umbrella. Should he feel any better dealing with you than with me?"

"Reckon not." He considered it for a moment before grinning faintly. "I reckon not. How's it feel to be worth more dead than alive?"

"I'm not used to the idea yet. And it won't be true until a year from now, when the probate court makes the transfer final. In the meantime, if you're right about Harrington, don't you think we should be keeping an eye out for some kind of reaction aimed at crippling the outfit financially before I get that far?"

"I see what you mean." Wing's hazel eyes had narrowed. "We got to hold the lid on, right? Watch ourselves?"

"Watch the jobs," I emphasized. "That's where we can be hurt. How do you feel about your crew?"

"The old timers I'll guarantee," he said immediately. "Shorty, Jerry, Bill Edwards, Willie—hell, they been with us since I used to borrow from one to pay another. No problem there. The newer ones—well, how can you be sure?"

"And we'll be hiring more for the Edmonds Road job," I pointed out. "Plenty of chances for Harrington to slip in a weasel or two on us."

"Yeah." Wing shook his head, then grinned suddenly. "Why'd you have to go an' load us up all of a sudden with these problems of wealth, pardner? When I been so used to cuttin' it as a poor man?" He had built himself up from the flatness of his mood when I'd given him the news. Wing always responded well to a challenge.

"Since the Edmonds Road job is bituminous instead of concrete," I continued, "and neither of us has given it a serious thought up to now, I'd better get back to the house and the drawing board and work out all the figures we'll need for the changeover. Drop by the house this evening and we'll kick the details around."

"Sure will." Wing sounded animated again. His glance had moved up the road where a T-shirted workman was balanced precariously over the big sluice gate of the paver, probing at a congestion in its mouth with a rake while a cement truck dumped its load into the capacious maw. "Lookit that idiot, will you?" He raised his voice. "Hey, you-all on the sluice! Git yore ass down from there less'n you want yore family to be tippin' their hats every time they drive down this stretch of road!"

A rumble of laughter swept through the crew, and the workman sheepishly backed away and stepped down to the ground. "Another thing, Wing," I said. He turned and looked at me. "How do you feel about Steve Curtin?"

"The county inspector? No ball of fire, but he's honest enough." Wing paused. "Or has been up to now. You think he could be bought?" I didn't answer. "Most can if the price is right," Wing answered himself. "Man, he could really put our tails in the gate if he started okayin' bad mix comin' out've the plant. 'Course, we usually run a doublecheck out here anyway—"

"From now on let's make it routine. And have the scales at the plant checked each night to make sure the interlocking device is working properly. A few pounds too much or too little of this or that could cost us some real money. And I mean check the scales when Curtin isn't around."

"You're really expectin' trouble, huh?" Wing sounded almost eager.

"I think Curtin might find temptation placed in his way. When has Tom Harrington ever taken a situation not to his liking lying down?" I didn't wait for Wing's answer. "Come on over to the house around eight."

"You bet, boss."

I walked back to the station wagon over the cushion of sand and three-eighths inch stone awaiting its overcoat of concrete. Properly wary, Wing wasn't going to let anyone put anything over on us out on the job sites. It was up to me to see that no one put anything over on us off them.

When I got back to the house, I found one letter in the mailbox. It was in an official-looking envelope. I opened it and took out a bill from the city's police department for towing my car from the Stardust Motel to the police lot. I readdressed the envelope to Chet Dorsey, care of City Hall, and put it back in the box for the mailman to pick up on his next round.

The telephone was ringing when I went inside. "Yes?" I said when I picked it up.

"I've been trying to reach you for an hour, Jim," Ludmilla Pierson said. "Drive over and have dinner with us."

Not 'will you or won't you' or 'can you or can't you', I thought. Just come. It was one of the things about Lud Pierson that had twisted my cork for years.

"George wants to talk to you," she added, as if reading my mind.

If George really wanted to talk to me, he'd have asked me to stop in at the bank. "Hold it a second, Lud," I said. "I just walked in and I'm running through the mail." I cupped a palm over the mouth of the receiver while I thought. There had been nothing special in her voice to indicate what she wanted; it could have been a social invitation except that from Ludmilla Pierson I didn't get them. There was nothing I could win talking to her. I uncovered the receiver. "There's a couple of letters I really should answer tonight, Lud—"

"Do you consider your financing on the upcoming Edmonds Road job important?" she interrupted.

"I guess I don't have to answer that one." What was the woman getting at? "Are you—"

"Come over and have dinner with us. You might learn something."

She hung up without waiting for a reply. Typical of her. I tested my beard growth with a knuckle while hanging up the phone. I decided to go, the clinching factor being that George would be present. I had plans for George. I'd watched Tom Harrington's operation carefully for two years now, and observed that he funneled his financing through a single banker most of the time, in his case, Bob Carmody of the Second National. I was aware that a contractor was a lot better off tying in with one bank and one banker than spreading all over the landscape; but operating on a shoestring the way we'd been, it just wasn't possible. If any one banker knew the shenanigans I'd gone through in the past four years to keep us afloat, I'd have been the poorest credit risk in Albermarle County.

I shed my clothes on the way upstairs, then showered and shaved. I rarely wear a tie, even on so-called dress occasions, and I didn't put one on this time. In our latitude, open-throated sportswear is at least semiformal attire, anyhow. I drove over and parked in the Pierson driveway, and George met me at the front door. Like Wing, his eyes lingered on my face. "Ran into a boom out on the job"—I forestalled the obvious question.

He nodded. "Sorry I had to disappoint you the other day, Jim," he said as we engaged in the perfunctory bankers' handshake. George is a stocky, round-faced man with steel-rimmed glasses shielding owlish eyes. I wondered if Lud had had anything to do with his

63

disappointing me, and whether the dinner invitation represented a change of heart on her part after she'd seen how I'd handled Harrington. George led the way into the living room, where Ludmilla reclined on a chaise longue in four ounces of green chiffon, looking every inch the Lady of the Manor. "Cocktail?" George asked me. "Martini? Manhattan?"

"Martini," I said.

"Dear?"

"Martini," Lud said. She was inspecting my face. "The most *interesting* things seem to be happening to you all the time, Jim."

"Now, dear," George said. He was already on his way over to a portable bar in a corner of the room. The ensuing silence was broken only by the clinking of bottles. Lud seemed to have nothing more to say, and I was saving my own *bons mots*. George advanced toward us, carrying the drinks carefully. In school I'd always thought him a lightweight, but rather a pleasant one. Seen up close, he seemed pompous. His sandy hair was already graying. Nothing like working in a bank to make a man look like a banker, I thought.

We had two drinks apiece before the housekeeper announced dinner. I tried steadily to get through to George conversationally, only to have Lud monopolize the small talk. One reason I'd asked for the appointment with George that he hadn't kept was the hope of sizing him up. If I was going to use him for the purpose I had in mind, I needed to know something more about him than the color of his socks. Whether Lud guessed my intention or not, she did a good job of stifling the leading questions I aimed across the table. Midway through dinner, George announced that he hated to be a member of the Eat-and-Run Club, but he had a previous engagement. That smacked of Lud's doing, too, and whatever was on her mind, I could do without. I decided to leave with George.

The dinner conversation convinced me of one thing; I was going to have to change my mind about using him. He'd always been around, but I'd never paid much attention to him. Watching him in action at his own table, it was obvious that there was nothing much to pay attention to. All through dinner, he never said "fire" 'til Lud said "hell." I've known men who could stand up to everyone in the world except their wives, but I couldn't give George the benefit of the doubt, even in that respect. He looked and sounded like an amiable jerk. He didn't even appear bright. For the life of me, I couldn't see how he could be expected to stand up to anyone in a tight business situation. I remembered Lud upstairs, with a briefcase full of papers, "doing George's homework for him." I didn't doubt it. What a hard-nosed type like her had ever seen in him to make her want to marry him in the first place was beyond me.

We adjourned to the library, and as I might have expected, Lud outmaneuvered me. I was just stretching my legs out comfortably with a pony of brandy in my fist when George spoke up. "I shouldn't be more than an hour, dear. Sorry to run out on you this way, Jim."

I gulped my brandy and started to rise from my chair, only to find Lud beside me refilling my glass. "Jim and I have a few items to discuss, anyway," she said.

"Another time," I said, and then I thought: What the hell? Why postpone it? I settled back into the chair. "I can spare you a few minutes."

"Thanks," she said drily. George had left the room without our being aware of it. Lud sat down in the high-backed chair opposite mine. Somehow it didn't dwarf her as it would have most women. She crossed her legs and went to work on her own brandy. With her skirt length what it was, it guaranteed me a flash of tanned thigh.

We sat and drank brandy silently for a time. Lud got up continually to keep our glasses filled. When conversation did ensue, it was elliptical, glancing off subjects without coming to grips with any of them. We had four brandies apiece before I tired of it. If she wanted to demonstrate she had a hollow leg, she could hire a hall. Despite the steel under her eggshell facade, she could hardly expect to drink me under the table head-to-head. I wondered if she was trying to loosen up my inhibitions. I wondered what made her think I had any. "Buttons off, Lud," I said. "What's on your mind?"

She smiled. She could have been drinking tea to that point except that I'd been watching it come from the same decanter. "What did you think of George?" she asked. "I saw you inspecting him during dinner."

"He's a nice fellow."

"Isn't he, though." There was no particular inflection in her voice, and she continued in the same tone. "I'm sure you know better than to come to dinner without a tie, Jim, so I can only consider the lack of one to be a deliberate affront to your hostess."

It raised my hackles. "For that particular hostess, I'm loaded with deliberate affronts."

She smiled again. "With the Edmonds Road job and the others you seem to think you'll be getting, you'll be moving in circles where a tie is *de rigueur*."

"Sorry I never studied Russian. Speaking of the Edmonds Road job—"

"I don't wish to speak of it."

"No? On the phone you said—"

"I don't care what I said on the phone." She was still smiling. She uncrossed her legs in a manner guaranteeing me a flash of untanned thigh, got up to refill our glasses again, and retreated to her chair.

"So?" I said impatiently. "What *do* you want to talk about, Lud?"

"George," she said. Her voice had turned husky, the only indication the brandy was having any effect on her. "But first, let's go upstairs and tie into each other. Just for fun."

"I'm not wearing a tie, remember? You like them couth, Lud." It made me curious, though. "Have you ever in your life had a real honest-to-John shagging? From a man who could make you say 'ouch'?"

Her smile was poised above the rim of her brandy pony. "You're applying for the position?"

"God forbid."

"I'm *so* disappointed." She took a slow swallow of

66

brandy. "Or should I feel relieved? At not having to confront your ravening masculinity?"

"Stop kittening it around, Lud," I said impatiently. "What's on your mind?"

"George," she said again. Her voice had turned lazy. "I want you to kill him for me."

"That's all?"

"No, that's not all. Then I want you to marry me."

The goddam woman means it, I thought. It's not the brandy talking. "Sorry," I said. "Both of those engagement books are filled right now."

She set down her glass carefully. "I want to run things in this county, Jim, but I need a man to do it. You saw for yourself that I'm not going to be able to reach the goal with George. If you take over from Harrington, and I'm surprised to find that I believe you will, you and I could make a winning team together. I'd bring you social and financial contacts you could never hope for otherwise."

"And a handy knife under the pillow."

Her smile was lopsided, but recognizable as such. "Wouldn't that merely add spice for a big he-man like you?" Her expression changed. "Wouldn't you like to get me on a bed, absolutely at your mercy?"

"I don't happen to think you've got the talent for the job."

Just for a second her claws showed. "*Damn* you! I'm better—" She chopped it off and immediately slipped back into her hostess veneer. "More brandy?"

I held out my glass, mainly to see if she could get up and walk. She could. "You don't seem to smarten up very fast about blackmailers," I went on. "How are you going to explain this interesting conversation to George when I play him the tape from the miniature recorder in my shirt pocket?"

That reached her, but the girl had a concrete gut; not a crack showed in the varnish of her composure. "*If* you had a recorder, which you haven't, I'd simply say I was plumbing the foulest depths of your foul nature." She grinned at me, pleased with herself.

"Okay, I haven't got a recorder," I agreed. "But I'm not taking on your propositions, either." I tried to move away from the subject. "I've got problems enough. Wing is mad at me, for one thing."

She was interested. "He is? Why?"

"He feels he's not carrying his share of the load, which is foolish."

"You men," she commented. But then she was right back at the other thing. "What I've said makes sense, Jim. For both of us."

"Thanks, but no."

"Are you afraid I might have a recorder in the room?"

"The thought did cross my mind."

"All right. Just keep on saying 'no.'" She rose to refill my glass again; I put my palm over the top of it. "But arrange an accident for him."

"Speaking of Wing, I asked him to be at my place at eight," I said. I looked at my watch, and it surprised me. "And it's now ten-fifteen. I'm leaving." I rose from my chair, and she followed me out to the front door. She was glassy-eyed, but she had yet to slur a syllable.

She put a hand on my arm as I opened the door. "An accident," she said urgently.

"You're out of the foulest depths of your foul mind, Lud," I said as I started down the walk to the station wagon.

As I was pulling out of the driveway, George Pierson pulled in, in an incongruous white T-bird. I glanced back at the house, but Lud had disappeared from the doorway. If they slept in the same bedroom, I wondered how she'd explain her brandy-laden aura. Although she wasn't the type to do much explaining.

I didn't lack for subjects to think about during the drive home.

When I pulled up in front of my house, Wing was sitting there in his car. He remained in it while I walked over to him; then he started in on me angrily. "The next time you tell *me* to come by your damn house at eight o'clock—"

"I had an unexpected dinner invitation, Wing."

"You couldn't have left a note? I wasted the whole damn evenin' waitin' on you."

From the sound of him I guessed that he'd had a whiskey bottle for company. "I forgot, that's all. I'm sorry." It sounded lame, even to me, but I couldn't understand his anger until his next words.

"I don't like the way you're actin', pardner. When you didn't show, I took a turn around town lookin' for the station wagon. An' guess where I found it parked? Your old friends ain't good enough for you, man?"

"It's business, Wing. We—"

"Don't you 'we' me, Jim." He turned on his ignition. "I haven't felt like a 'we' in our setup for longer'n I like to think about." He gunned the motor viciously. "An' from the looks of things, it don't feel to me like I'm goin' to." He slammed into the accelerator and roared away in a squeal of tires.

The measure of his anger was the measure of the loss of camaraderie in our personal relationship. Four months ago he'd have cheerfully waited out a weekend. All too well I knew the hurt pride of a man like Wing. But what could I do?

I locked up the station wagon and went into the house.

CHAPTER V

I STEPPED into the drugstore pay phone and reached for my change. For no good reason at all I felt fine; I felt loose as ashes. I dialed the seven-digit number and listened to the ring at the other end of the line. "Victor Cartwright's office," Veronica Peters said.

"How'd you like to have your pants taken down to-night, Veronica?" I asked her. "Not for the same reason your old man used to take them down?"

"Approval of the matter in which you're interested appears to be merely a question of time, Mr. Jackson," she replied.

"Mr. Jackson" was the signal that someone was sitting in the anteroom, within hearing distance, waiting for Vic, and that she couldn't speak freely. "And have your belly rubbed?" I continued.

"Nothing out of the ordinary has been noted in your proposal, sir."

"And your butt rousted all over a king-sized bed?"

"I believe I'm quite safe in saying that your proposition meets with general approval, Mr. Jackson."

"And your curls braided?"

"The—ah—details of the indicated course of action promise to be quite satisfactory."

"Rowley's at six-thirty?"

"That will be fine, sir."

"Bring flesh, Veronica. Heated."

"Oh, that's easily managed, sir. You have no idea of the present status in that regard."

"Six-thirty."

"I've made a note of it. And thank you for calling, sir."

I hung up the phone.

I was ten minutes early reaching Rowley's back parking lot, but Veronica was there before me. "I'm going to have an accident someday when you talk to me like that on the phone," she greeted me.

"You like to hear about it, puss?"

"Well—part of me does and part of me doesn't. Does that make sense?"

"Perfectly. Let's go."

She transferred to the station wagon, and we drove to the cabin. Veronica took several deep inhalations of the soft air under the pine trees. "It's so nice out here, Jim," she said when I unlocked the door and we went inside. "I know we've had some good times at my place, but I was never able to fully relax there. I was always waiting for the phone to ring, or someone to knock on the door, or—well, there was always a knot in my stomach that never seemed to dissolve completely."

"Never?"

70

She laughed. "Only when the noncerebral part of me took over. And never for very long, unfortunately. Here, I feel"—she flung out an arm—"well, *relaxed*."

"You have me curious to see what form this new-found feeling of relaxation is going to take."

We were in the larger bedroom, facing each other. She put her arms around my neck and drew my face down to hers. When she removed her lips from mine, she unbuttoned my shirt and pulled its tails from my belt. Her expression was sweetly serious as she unbuckled and unzipped my trousers. She guided them downward, and I stepped out of them. She slipped down my shorts and placed my apparatus on her warm palm. "Stretch out on the bed," she whispered. "I'll be right with you." She hesitated. "Can I be the engineer?"

"Be my guest."

Her hands went to the tiny loops at the back of the neck of her dress, then paused. It seemed she had other preparations to make first. I sat on the bed and removed shoes, socks, and undershirt while she went to the bureau, dragged it alongside the bed, then angled its mirror downward so I could see myself in it. She undressed quickly. Crease marks from her underwear were faintly visible on the undersides of her big, firm breasts, around her waist, and across her upper thighs.

"Let me do it all," she breathed, joining me on the bed.

I found it no hardship to let her do it all.

Her preliminary arrangements made to her satisfaction, she turned her head to consider the slow undulations of her own milky flesh in the mirror. She went from a languorous glide to a plunging attack to a slow-motion diminuendo before subsiding altogether. For a few seconds our rapid breathing intermingled; then I reached around and slapped a sleek haunch. Obediently she slipped down beside me. "*Aaaahhh*, that was good," she said quietly. Her eyes were closed.

Granted that this girl had a lively curiosity and a healthy aptitude for bedroom acrobatics, why should a session with her be so incomparably better than it had ever been with Mona? I had no real feeling for

71

Veronica; she was a nice kid, and a superlatively good lay, but there it was. There'd been at least one time in my life when I was in love with Mona, if I knew the meaning of the word. I'd broken my neck with her to achieve and give just a part of the satisfaction attained so effortlessly with this plump redhaired girl, and I had been met by total indifference. Indifference at first, followed by increasingly irritating slurs.

It didn't make sense.

Still on my back, with Veronica's even breathing warming my shoulder, I stared up at the ceiling . . .

We'd been married about a year when Mona and I went to one of the Saturday night dances at the country club. It was the usual sort of thing: a lot of drinking, strolls in the garden by mismatched husbands and wives, and occasional disappearances by same. There was damned little dancing. Mona sat at our table for hours with the same warm beer in front of her and the same cool smile on her face, so fixed that it must have hurt her ears. She didn't want to dance. She didn't want to drink. She wanted to sit there feeling sorry for herself. Why? I was never able to extract a reason. I sat there drinking for us both.

The Moline Country Club incorporates several social strata in its membership. People rub elbows there who never meet anywhere else in town. Mona's gaze lingered longest on the Pierson table, where Ludmilla, resplendent in a floor-length gown, presided over a changing coterie of admiring males while George beamed fatuously and smoked a cigar. Ludmilla had shed her usual chilly demeanor to become the belle of the ball. Wing Darlington danced with her twice, his maghogany-tinted blondness complementing her silvery sheen.

Mona, resplendent also in a floor-length gown whose cost I'd spent a third of the evening estimating, rose abruptly to her feet. "I want to go home," she announced. It was a familiar gambit. I started to argue, then changed my mind. In a year, I'd learned I couldn't win any arguments. If I came out ahead on points on a technicality, I was saddled with a silent martyr around the house for a week. I hadn't the temperament that could afford such victories.

On the ride home, her mood could fairly be described as sulky. "What was the matter tonight?" I opened with the Ruy Lopez. "You wanted to go."

"I have a headache."

"I don't mind your not dancing with me, but when you refuse fellows like George Pierson and Charlie—"

"I said I have a headache!"

There were no surprises in the dialogue. It was like a high school play in which everyone knew everyone else's lines. At home, Mona shed her clothes just inside the front door and began to prowl restlessly through the house. She had this thing about stalking pantherishly through all the rooms, upstairs and down, naked. She had on earrings with dangling pendants, a double strand of pearls, and blood-red, high-heeled dancing pumps.

I was at the liquor cabinet when she passed me on one of her circuits, the dimpled, high-pointed cheeks of her behind twinkling. I reached out and took her by the arm. She stopped and went into her act; without quite collapsing, she became as limp as it's possible for a person to be and still remain upright. She had a trick of becoming as boneless as an eel. Opposition I like; cooperation I love; compliance I detest. Mona fed me compliance in a steady dose. The first time, she rose from our bed with the single comment "Messy!" I almost hit her. It might have been better if I had.

I let go her arm, and she went upstairs. I had two fast drinks that demolished the bottle's contents and went to bed in the downstairs bedroom. It was the first time, but not the last.

Two years of it drove me to a psychiatrist in Wilmington. He hadn't wanted to see me, but a friend wangled it. The psychiatrist was a lean man with watery-looking eyes behind heavy glasses. "I have your check, but I haven't cashed it," he began when I sat down across from him at his desk. "This can't do any good.

Nothing constructive can emerge from a generalized twenty-minute interview."

"You said all that on the phone, Doc," I said. "I'm trying to get a picture. I'm not making it with my wife, and I'd like to know why."

He sighed, then leaned back in his chair, fixing his eyes on a point somewhere above my left shoulder. "I'm not even the best psychiatrist you can find," he went on. "Merely the best you can afford. And catch-as-catch-can opinions are notoriously dangerous. If I saw you for a year, and your wife for the same length of time, I might possibly be able to tell you something that would help you with your problem." He cleared his throat. "An opinion ventured on insufficient data might be the worst thing I could do for you."

"Let me worry about that, Doc."

He placed his hands on the desk top, palms down. I was surprised to see that he bit his fingernails. "Are you potent?"

"Yes."

"With your wife?"

"So far."

"Are you oversexed?"

"I don't think so."

"From what do you derive your greatest sexual pleasure?"

"Ramming it home."

"You're a big man. Your hands are calloused. You admit to an impatient attitude. Do you consider yourself sadistic in your lovemaking?"

"I've had women tell me I was rough. I never had one refuse to try it again."

"What is a typical behavior pattern in a sex situation with your wife?"

"Me charging and her like a rag doll."

"Always?"

"Since about a month after we were married."

"Did you engage in premarital intercourse?"

"Twice."

"Satisfactorily?"

74

"No, but I thought it was because of inexperience. She was a virgin."

His eyes came down from their point-in-space vacant stare over my shoulder and settled on my face. "Scarcely the commonest commodity these days."

"She was a virgin."

"She has men friends?"

I'd been watching his hands drumming on the desk top. I looked at him. "Not really, if you mean does she run around. My friends come to the house—"

"Women friends?"

"A few. Two or three."

"Hen parties?"

I started to say "Yes" automatically, then stopped and thought. "Well, no, I guess not. She doesn't play bridge—"

"Does she ever fight you off in the sex act?"

"No."

"But she derives no gratification from it?"

"If she does, she's an actress at hiding it."

"What gives her pleasure?"

"Sexual pleasure? Nothing. With me, anyway. Unless you'd say she gets pleasure from parading through the house in her skin, waving it at me, then turning as dead as Kelsey's nuts when I go after it."

"You've stopped going after it?"

"Almost."

The incisive questions continued for a solid thirty-five minutes. I told that man things I'd never fully admitted to myself. The sweat poured off me. And finally he sat back in his chair, shaking his head. He opened a drawer, took out my check, and pushed it across the desk to me. "I can't do you any good," he said. "I'm not an M.D. who can say 'Take a yellow pill.'"

The check remained in the center of the desk between us. "Is it me, Doc?"

"I haven't seen your wife," he pointed out. "I believe you tried to be honest in your responses, but in that area people rarely are, at least not completely. That's why repeated sessions are recommended."

"Is it me?"

"There is a pattern," he began; then he stopped. "Basically you seem an uncomplicated individual," he resumed. "With perhaps an overcompensatory drive a certain type of woman might find repugnant."

"A certain type of woman?"

He hesitated again. "Snap judgement, and not valid. But a woman with a bit less than average interest in men."

"It doesn't sound fatal, Doc."

"It needn't be. I'd recommend counseling for you both, however." He slapped his hands down on the desk top. "That's it, Mr. Wilson. I've probably done you no favor with an off-the-cuff interpretation of what in the ultimate case could be a deep-seated traumatic condition or a comparatively simple case of maladjustment. If you'd come to me from anyone other than whom you did, I'd not have gone this far. And I'd suggest a decent measure of restraint in any course of action you contemplate taking."

I left his office still not sure.

It was another year before I was sure.

Veronica rolled over against me and blew gently on my neck. "I have to get dressed," she said.

"Let's stay here tonight," I suggested. I placed a palm in the center of the inverted bowl of her substantial belly and rotated the palm briskly. White flesh danced in rippling waves. "I'll run up the road and pick up a couple of fried chickens and a case of beer. We'll have an orgy. I'll swipe some grapevine leaves for garlands."

She was watching her own gelatinous vibrations in the bureau mirror. "I'd love to, Jim, but I told—ooooh, stop it!—I told Mr. Cartwright I'd come back to the office tonight for some special dictation."

"You're the stinky type who puts business before pleasure?"

She laughed. "I'm a working gal."

"Hardworking," I agreed. I leaned up over her. "Care to give another demonstration?"

76

"Love to."

"Which charm school taught you not to press a gentleman for a reengagement?"

"The school of soft thumps," she said demurely.

We went to work, and in each ensuing movement of the waltz, Veronica met me just a little better than halfway. She was a *première danseuse*. "I'll turn on the shower for you," I said a few minutes later, and I left the bedroom to do so. When I returned, she was still on the bed, stretching luxuriantly. "What's so important about the dictation tonight?" I asked, dropping down on the bed beside her.

"Nothing, really, except that with Mr. Cartwright out of the office two days a week, we're falling behind with the routine work." She sat up reluctantly, swung her legs over the edge of the bed, and stood up.

I wrenched my attention from the sight of my fingerprints in her tail to a fuller appreciation of her words. "Why should Vic be out of the office a couple of days each week?"

"I thought I'd told you. Mr. Harrington is using him in Spartanburg on some kind of job." She stooped quickly, kissed me, then trotted to the bathroom, jiggling pleasantly.

I stared after her for a moment before dropping back on the pillow with my hands behind my head. This business about Cartwright's spending so much time in Spartanburg—not for the first time did I wonder if Ludmilla Pierson could have known that the blackmailer came from Spartanburg. If she did, and had told Harrington—although how could she without revealing the source of her information, namely herself? It didn't seem likely, but it wouldn't hurt to get a line on Harrington's interest.

"Is Harrington interested in the Blackwood subdivision over in Spartanburg?" I asked casually when Veronica came back into the bedroom.

"I don't know," she replied as her hips disappeared into her panties. "Mr. Cartwright never mentions what he's doing there."

"No dictation on Spartanburg?"

"None. So far, anyway."

It was hardly the type of answer to leave me feeling overconfident.

I dashed in and out of the shower, dressed, and drove Veronica back to her car.

The next three weeks were as busy as any I'd ever put in. Except for one date with Veronica, I stuck to cost-sheet estimates and material-quantity breakdowns. I spent a lot of time also with suppliers and subcontractors. Wing and I had handicapped ourselves by getting off on the wrong foot on the Edmonds Road job. Not only was it five or six times more extensive than any we'd taken on before, but our original bid, made at a time when we hadn't a prayer of getting the job, had been made on a superficial analysis of the problems. Since we hadn't been low bidder, I wasn't afraid of losing money; as far as economy went, I was sure we could match performance with anyone. But since this was our first big slice of pie, I wanted to wring all the water out of the job costs to make sure some of the money stuck to us.

Wing's attitude remained surly during my trips out to Sunset Lane to confer with him. I ignored it because I was sure he'd come around. Although I felt that most of his feeling of dissatisfaction was based on my recent outmaneuvering of Tom Harrington without awarding Wing what he considered an appropriate role to play, part of our trouble went back considerably beyond that. Wing couldn't accept his own limitations. He was a hell of a good construction superintendent, but he started and stopped right there. He had a much better relationship with our work crews than I ever did; he could jolly them along. I'm no jollier. A road doesn't get paved only at the job site, though, and almost from the beginning of the partnership, I'd carried more than my share of the preparatory load. Originally, the division of labor between us called for Wing to be our liaison with suppliers who, being human, had a way of trying to take advantage of a small operator. After Wing blew his stack and tipped their desks over on a couple of these people, it was agreed that I'd take over that aspect of the work, too. Not that my temper was any better than Wing's; it was just that I'd learned to smile—and wait.

When we were only ten days away from the completion of the Sunset Lane job and the changeover from concrete to bituminous, I took my job breakdown across the state to a man whose judgement I trusted. On a big paving job, a firm doesn't get any second guesses, none they can afford to live with, anyway. Bill Moore was a retired contractor who'd given me my first job out of college. He was a self-made man, tough and shrewd. He went over my figures carefully, and finally tossed his pencil aside. "It looks all right," he said. "If you're sure you're not running into anything more than a heavy clay base."

"I'm sure. I drilled the test holes myself."

He nodded, studying the specifications sheet. "Ten-inch sand cushion, six-inch gravel coating, two-and-a-half inch stone topped by three-eighths-inch stone, two inches of asphalt—" His voice died away as he leaned back in his chair. "Who's doing your financing?"

"Are you volunteering, Bill?"

He smiled and shook his head. "If I wanted to risk my money, I'd still be in the game myself."

"Fair enough. I've got six or eight people I've been using right along that I can go to. I'll hit them harder this time, and more of them. I don't anticipate—" I stopped. Moore was shaking his head. "What's the matter?"

"This is a big job, Jim. You can't afford to nickel and dime it like that. It hurts your image. One of the hardest things to learn in this business is to start thinking big enough to avoid being a little man all your life. You've got to promote yourself a real line of credit. It shouldn't be a problem, since it's a county job and everyone knows the money is good."

"But the county takes its own sweet time about

paying, Bill. If I sign a paper with a bank, they want their money at 3:00 P.M. of the designated day. I'd rather do business with people I can go to and say 'Jack, I'm going to stand you off another ninety days on that loan.' "

"I appreciate your thinking because I started out that way myself, Jim, but from where you stand now it's all wrong. You're going to be bidding on work in the future where the first thing the prime party will want to know is your bank reference. What are you going to tell them? Sand Hill Bank on Shadyside Lane? What you need is a friendly banker, one who knows the problems of the business and is prepared to go along with you."

"I don't know any friendly bankers."

"Naturally. You never had anything to offer them before. Go talk to a couple now. You might be surprised."

So after the drive back home, I dropped in to see George Pierson. He was cordial and heard me out, then removed his glasses and polished them carefully. "Ludmilla thought you'd be in about this, Jim," he said. "Why don't you run out to the house and talk to her about it?"

It took me a minute to get it. "You mean you, personally, can't make the decision?"

It didn't faze him a bit. "Different areas of a bank's operation require different viewpoints, Jim."

I wondered if his area consisted of counting the postage stamps. This was the banker I'd considered using when I took over from Harrington? I must need bifocals. I got to my feet. "Thanks for listening, George."

He walked with me to the door of his office. "Talk to Lud, Jim. She has a good head on her shoulders for that sort of thing." He was totally unembarrassed at the admission of his own incapacity. It takes all kinds to make a world.

I took a couple of days to think it over. I wasn't anxious to put my head in that particular lioness' mouth. Still, everything Bill Moore had said made sense. We couldn't penny-ante along forever. And if I went to an out-of-town bank, the first thing they'd want to know was why the local bank wasn't accommodating me. I called Lud, finally, and arranged to see her. I'd had so much on my mind recently that it wasn't until I pulled into the Pierson driveway that I recalled the details of my last visit. After the load of brandy she'd taken on, I wondered how many of the details Lud recalled.

She received me in her upstairs sitting room; she was surrounded by little stacks of paper on the floor around her chair. Her peach-colored dress was cut low under the arms, and she was wearing her glasses, which oddly made her look younger. If I hadn't known her, she'd have looked good to me.

"George said you'd been in to see him." She started the ball rolling. "What's the total figure you'll need to swing the job without wondering where your next payroll is coming from?"

"Three hundred seventy-five thousand."

She reached down to pick up one of the piles of paper, and I could see a very pretty bulge of breast. "I have a figure here forty-five thousand higher than that," she said.

"We cut corners, Lud. We try harder."

She didn't smile. "The credit could be arranged."

"It could? What would it cost us?"

She waved a hand. "Standard charges. You couldn't do any better. This method of financing, though, is not the way I'd prefer to see you get the money."

"No?"

"No. What have you done about the proposition we discussed the other night?"

"Which proposition was that?"

"You know which proposition. If you were married to me, Jim, financing could hardly be a problem."

"You forget that I saw George in action at the bank. I don't care for the jobs you get your husbands."

"You're not George, for God's sake." She rose from her chair and paced the room impatiently. "Can't you understand, Jim? It could be a big thing for us. Ever since I was a little girl, I've wanted to be a part of the power elite in the state. I had a good start with the family money, but I needed a man. I thought I could make George into the man, but you saw what happened to

81

that idea. You have more rough edges than a shagbark hickory tree, and they'd have to be planed down before you could pass in the type of society we'd be entertaining, but it could be managed." I opened my mouth to tell her I didn't care for her managing, but she continued right on. "We could be married three months after George has his accident. We could even—"

"Three months!"

"Well, four or five. What's the difference? People are going to talk, anyway. Then someone runs off with someone else's wife and we'd be out of the public eye again. And we'd have what we wanted."

"You'd have what you wanted."

"All right, let's get down to cases. What would *you* want?"

"From you, nothing. If George is bugging you so badly, Lud, why don't you divorce him?"

"There'd be too many loose ends if he were still around."

"You mean it might cost you a few dollars?"

"There'd be too many loose ends," she repeated.

"About the loan, Lud—"

She shook her blonde head. "You're talking business, and I'm talking success—power. Can't you see it, Jim? You're going to take Harrington—he's ripe to be taken. I can see it now that you've pointed it out. Together we could run the state, Jim."

"I'll admit it, Lud: you're too fast for me. I can't keep up with your thinking. Just tell me 'Yes' or 'No' on the loan."

"Oh, you can have it."

"Okay, then. I'll be leaving now."

She offered no objection but walked downstairs with me. "I thought you showed me something a while back, but I guess it was just a flash in the pan," she said as I went out the front door.

"I save my energy for pulling my own chestnuts out of the fire," I told her as I went down the walk.

I thought it was a silly conversation. The only good thing I'd heard in it was that she thought I was going to take Harrington. As long as she kept on thinking it, it should make her less interested in Spartanburg, assuming Spartanburg had been her idea originally. I must remember to get Veronica to root around in Vic Cartwright's private files and see what the hell was going on in Spartanburg. I didn't like loose ends any better than Lud did.

The next day, I saw George at the bank and filled in and signed about twenty-two forms giving my pedigree, financial and otherwise. I stuffed a batch of them into a folder to take to Wing to sign, too. There is no shortage of paper work in banks. "I'd say two weeks," George replied when I asked how long clearance would take.

A week later, I was driving home at night with the car radio on. I was thinking about Wing. He'd signed the papers all right, but morosely. I was going to have to do something to get him back to the good-natured, roughhouse, kidding attitude that was an integral part of him usually and had been so noticeably missing recently. The news announcer's half-heard words jolted me into a state of awareness. "—high rate of speed. The car was totally demolished. Mr. Pierson was thirty-two years old and vice-president of the Commonwealth Bank. Funeral arrangements have not yet been completed."

I pulled the car over to the side of the road and stopped. After a minute, I turned off the radio.

It was quite a while before I restarted the engine and continued the drive home.

CHAPTER VI

GEORGE PIERSON'S DEATH left me in a position with Lud where I didn't know whether to back up or go ahead. Instinct told me to grab the cow by the udders; caution argued that my stance was poor. In the end, I did nothing but go to the funeral, as half the town did. If I was right in my estimate of the situation, I'd be hearing from Lud without any necessity on my part for pushing the issue.

I heard in a week. She called the house one afternoon when I was enmeshed in a maze of figures. I didn't even recognize her voice. "Oh," I said finally. "Lud. Yes. What d'you want?" The second it was out I realized that the tone of complete unawareness could only be considered lese majesty.

As it was. "I want you to come out to the house," Lud said, slivers of ice crackling in every syllable.

All the former imperiousness was back in her voice. I was tempted to give her an argument—it had been that kind of day—but there didn't seem to be any point in it. "I'll be over," I said. I hung up my T-square and went out front to the station wagon.

As I drove over to the Pierson house my thoughts weren't pleasant. Until he was gone, I hadn't realized what a buffer George Pierson had been between me and Lud. Despite her high-and-mighty indifference to public opinion, there were things even she couldn't do. The number of these had been sharply diminished, and I didn't care for the prospect of the consequences.

She received me in a black dress, whose color was its only concession to mourning. I could have spit through the fabric, which clung to her like wax to linoleum. "I've had a discreet investigation made," she began without preliminary when we were installed in her upstairs sitting room. "There's no question about it. Someone tampered with the steering knuckle on George's Thunderbird."

"We both know you didn't need an investigation to find that out, Lud."

She ignored it. "Facts have emerged that could lead the authorities to want to ask you some questions. If the facts were called to their attention."

"Oh, I see. *I* killed George, is that it? Do you mind telling me my motive?"

"Revenge because he had turned down your application for a line of credit."

84

That reached me. "Turned down—? What the hell are you talking about? George *okayed* my application."

"You have it in writing, of course?"

"Of course." I bluffed.

She smiled. "You must be a formidable poker player. George never signed anything before I looked over the details."

The woman had had her husband killed. It would have made a lot of sense to her to arrange the facts so the evidence pointed toward me. "So?"

"So unless you marry me, I'm prepared to turn over the results of my investigation to the authorities."

It probably should have had a greater impact on me than it did. I couldn't stand a noise like this; my current odor in the community was bad enough. All I felt was irritation, though. "Why don't you get off that button, Lud? If it's a good jabbing you want, I'll line up a half dozen young bucks for you, one for every night in the week."

She refused to take the needle. "Much as I detest you personally, it's you I want to marry. I need your ruthlessness to move ahead with plans I've had for years."

My ruthlessness? That was a good one. I made another try; if I could get her mad enough, I might yet see daylight on this. "Why bother me with trivialities now? All I'm interested in is the line of credit. Everything is ready to go—"

"*If* you marry me, there'll be no difficulty about the credit," she interrupted. "If you don't, there'll be nothing but. You can't obtain it from us now, anyway." She smiled again. "Since that would permit you to name me as an accessory after the fact if I later had to use the revenge motif as substantiation for your killing him. The people who count know, you see, that if George refused you, it was with my knowledge. So I could hardly grant you the credit later, could I? Without being vulnerable?" She leaned back in her chair and considered me. "But assuming you agree to cooperate, I've already made other arrangements—quiet arrangements—for you to get the money."

The damn woman thought of everything. "Do you think this town is going to hold still for the kind of three ring circus you're suggesting, Lud? You're underestimating—"

"A nine days' wonder," she said briskly. "Who's to question it? Seriously? And what do we care what the public thinks or says? No, there's no problem."

"But why get married, for God's sake? I can bulldoze just as many people for you without living under the same roof."

"There are several reasons. In the area we're both interested in, a woman without a husband can't reach the type of men I want to listen to me. A woman with a rough, tough, nasty husband gets an excellent hearing, especially if he has financial and political weight to add to his avoirdupois. With the muscle we'll have to go with your nerve"—she paused to regard me over the tops of her glasses—"if you haven't lost it, we're going to own this end of the state." She said it with complete confidence.

I had no great respect for public opinion myself. In different circumstances, and if Lud had been anyone but who she was, I might have jumped at the chance. She had looks and brains. She represented money and power. But—she was Ludmilla Pierson, and I'd known her for years.

As usual, she was thinking right along with me. "When you think it over, Jim, you'll have more reasons for wanting to than I do. We can be married in four months. Say the end of December." Another quick smile. "Mustn't forget the tax advantages. And meanwhile, a truce to all the sniping. You've got the credit, and you can go ahead with the job."

I was groping for something to slow her down with. "What do you think Tom Harrington would have to say about your marrying me?"

"I stopped worrying about what Tom Harrington had to say the day I was in his office with you," she said crisply.

If it was a fight, I'd lost every round of it. I decided to

86

get out while I was still alive. "I'll be running along, Lud."

"Start dropping by the house evenings," she said, swinging herself up from her reclining chair in a swirl of diaphanous skirt that revealed sleek legs. "We should have a proper courtship, you know. I'll let you know which evenings."

I choked down a reply. She was too confident, and I had to find out why before I tackled her head on. At best, she should have figured our situation as a stalemate; we each had something on the other. She was acting, though, as if she were completely in the driver's seat, and it might not be just her natural cussedness.

She didn't follow me downstairs; and getting into the station wagon, I looked back at the house.

When I was in the upstairs sitting room, it appeared that Lud had thought of everything. Sitting in the car, I wondered if that were true. If I couldn't think of an angle, and if she pushed me hard enough—

One thing was clear: if Ludmilla Pierson had a fatal accident, the last stone was off my back and I was home free.

I called Vic Cartwright's office from my house later that afternoon. "Veronica?"

"Yes, Mr. Jackson?"

"What's the chance of your getting into Vic's file and finding out for me what he's up to in Spartanburg?"

"That's the most difficult request you've ever made of this office, sir."

"He keeps it locked all the time?"

"That's right. It is."

"But you must need to get into it occasionally?"

"Rarely. And usually with supervision."

"One time is all I need, baby. It could be worth a couple of dollars to me to know."

She hesitated. "It will be difficult, sir. I don't see how—"

"For the home team, Veronica."

"Well—I'll put it at the top of the list." She still sounded doubtful. "Don't expect too much."

"You'll find a way."

"I honestly don't see how. Without—without—you know I'm not retiring soon, sir."

"Don't worry about Vic firing you. I'd like an excuse to line him up in front of the firing squad, anyway."

"You couldn't get along without it?"

"It would mean a great deal to me if you found out."

"Well—"

"You'll find a way," I repeated.

She didn't reply, and I hung up. Veronica promised to be no exception that people were wonderful until asked for something, but I had a feeling she'd come through. Even though she hadn't thanked me for calling this time.

I stood there in the front hall, conscious suddenly of the sticky, late afternoon heat. I went upstairs and took a shower, then came back down in slippers, slacks and T-shirt. I went into the kitchen and built myself a collins in the tallest glass I could find, then carried it outside to the patio, which was shaded at that hour by a butternut tree.

The kitchen's sterile, unused appearance reminded me of the womanless state of the house. I ought to get someone in to clean on a regular basis. I'm neat enough—Mona used to be amused at my obsession about a place for everything and everything in its place; she lived in a discarded-clothing-on-the-floor atmosphere—and I'd made several tours of the house with vacuum and dust mop, but a home gets a frowsy look without some serious housekeeping to keep it licked into shape. Not that Mona was ever a serious housekeeper, but she had kept a sharp eye on the various maids she'd brought in to do the work. None of them had ever lasted long on the job. I was continually coming home and running into a new one.

I sat down on a flimsy wickerwork chair on the patio, put my feet up on another, dipped my bill into the collins, and settled down to some serious thinking. The afternoon's conversation with Lud had been disturbing because it had crystallized a few half-formed notions that had been floating about in the back of my skull. It wasn't her monomania about marriage that bothered me; I'd deal with that situation in its own good time. No; the item that had been looming larger and larger ever since I'd heard the radio report of George Pierson's "accident" was the identity of the man she'd conned into tampering with the steering mechanism of George's car.

Granted she'd planned it, but she hadn't crawled under the car and done it herself. Someone had done it for her, and I very much needed to know the name of the gentleman. An unknown, sharp-edged cutting tool like that was a dangerous commodity in the neighborhood, especially if she took a notion to turn it loose against me at some time in the future. I had to find out who had done it for her, and the sooner the better.

She wouldn't have tried to hire a professional; that would have opened her again to the same sort of blackmail deal that had already scorched her patrician butt. It almost had to be somebody local, on whom she had a hold of some kind. With the bank behind her, a lot of people were obligated to her in one way or another, but how many would have the nerve and skill to bring off such a coup? It took a certain amount of mustard, even granted the attractiveness with which she could festoon the deal. I wondered if her fair white body had been a part of the contract. If it had, the guy had been a big loser on that end of the proposition, at least.

I thought myself around in circles right down to the bottom of the collins glass, and got exactly nowhere. I couldn't think of anyone's being obligated to Lud and having the chilled-steel nerve requisite for loosening the steering knuckle of a man's car, leaving it operating by a thread. I gave up the problem in disgust, finally. When I glanced around the yard, I was surprised to find that dusk had enveloped the patio. I realized suddenly that I was hungry.

I went to the garage to get out the portable charcoal grill. As I rolled up the door, I was brought up short by the sight of Mona's Pontiac. I'd had it driven in from where she'd left it the afternoon she'd met Whit Bailey. I wasn't supposed to dispose of any of her property until

89

the probate court made the settlement final, but in a year, the car would depreciate more than its book value by standing idle. I'd have to find out from whom I needed permission to sell it.

Looking at the Pontiac reminded me that I'd never checked it out for her personal belongings. I opened the door and took the keys out of the ignition, then went around to the rear and opened the trunk. It was empty except for the spare tire. Next I tried the locked glove compartment. There was nothing in it but a shriveled-up candy bar and the automobile insurance policy that went with the car. One reason I'd been able to proceed against her with confidence was that we'd had only one small policy on her life and I'd quietly let that lapse eighteen months ago. I locked up the Pontiac and put the keys in my pocket.

I rolled the grill out onto the patio, dumped a load of charcoal into it, squirted a stream of starter fluid onto the lumps, and ignited it. I went into the kitchen and took a slab of steak and a stick of butter from the refrigerator, greased the steak, salted and peppered it liberally, and slid it onto a platter. Then I carried it back out to the patio to wait until my charcoal was ready. It was dark enough then, so I turned on the patio lights. The back edge of my property ran through to the next street, and recently I'd rearranged my outside lights so that they would illumine the outer edges of the patio and the walk beyond and leave the near side of the house itself in comparative darkness. I'd considered installing a spotlight whose beam would have reached to the back gate, but decided against it. The neighbors had enough to talk about now.

I lit a cigarette and settled down in the wickerwork chair. The houses on both sides of mine were quiet. Although the patio was almost dark, a faint glow of sunset remained in the western sky. The silence was broken by a metallic ping, a sound I recognized as the aluminum gate on the back street side of my Anchor fence being opened. I rolled out of my chair and crouched be-

hind the grill, wishing I were in the bedroom, where my
.38 was.

A slim figure in a white sport shirt moved leisurely up
the path. It stopped just outside the bright limits of my
patio lights, and I strained my eyes trying to see who it
was. "Wilson!" a voice called softly.

I didn't say anything.

"Wilson!" the voice repeated. The voice had an urgent
sound. "I'm goin' to walk into the light an' turn around
so you can see I'm clean." After a deliberate pause, the
blurred figure did so. I still didn't recognize the man, but
clad as he was in nearly form-fitting slacks and shirt, it
was obvious he carried no armament. I came out from
behind the grill. "Glad I caught you at home," the man
continued. "Satisfied with my looks?"

"I'm satisfied."

He covered the remainder of the distance between us
in a deliberate manner and held out his hand. "Sam Carstens," he said, introducing himself. His handshake was
muscular. "Richie Hoey thought it might be a good idea
if I dropped in an' said hello."

"By the back gate?"

Carstens grinned. "Richie don't favor publicity none."

Richie Hoey was the chief of a county fief two hundred miles from Moline, where he operated very much
as Tom Harrington had locally. Carstens was sandy-
haired, and had a scattering of freckles. There was a
reckless tinge to his grin. His name rang a faint bell;
it seemed to me I should remember something about a
Sam Carstens, but it didn't come to mind. I glanced at
the grill; the charcoal was a glowing red. "I was just about
to drop a steak on that," I said. "Join me?"

"Don't mind 'f I do, Wilson."

I slid the steak from the platter onto the grill above
the coals, and it began sizzling immediately. I turned
back to Carstens. "Drink?"

"Fine."

"Gin?"

"Or whatever."

"Bourbon?"

"Reckoned you'd get around to it," the sandy-haired man said comfortably. He settled down in a leisurely manner in the next chair to mine. I went into the kitchen again to make the drinks. After carrying them out to the patio, I made another round trip for plates, knives, and forks. When handing Carstens his bourbon-and-branch, I'd noticed a tracery of fine, white-ridged scars on his left forearm. Back at the grill, I turned the steak over and poured the drippings from the catch-pan back over the meat. "How d'you like yours, Sam?"

"Anyway a-tall when I get it like this." He grinned.

"Rare?"

"Suits fine."

I tested the steak by slicing a corner; then I forked it onto the platter. After carrying it to the table, I cut it through the center and tipped each half onto the plates. I pushed a plate and half of the silverware over to Carstens' side of the table. "Eat up, Sam."

"Right nice of you, Wilson," he replied, pulling his chair closer.

The conversation lapsed. I was half a dozen bites into my own steak before I noticed that Carstens had ignored the knife I'd brought out from the kitchen for him. He was using a bone-handled, long-bladed pocketknife to cut his steak. As I watched him slice the red meat effortlessly, it came to me where I'd heard his name before. Sam Carstens was a knife fighter, and one with a reputation. The network of scars on his left, or guard, forearm should have indicated it to me. Rumor had it that Carstens had killed at least one man with the knife he now used so tranquilly to slice his steak.

Finished, he leaned back in his chair with a repleted sigh and went to work on his front teeth with a soiled toothpick extracted from a shirt pocket. "Nothin' personal in anything I bring up now," he began when the tooth cleaning ritual had been completed to his satisfaction. "What I got to say is strictly business." He was cleaning his knife very carefully with a corner of his handkerchief; I had forgotten to supply napkins. He folded the knife and slipped it into his pocket, eyeing me appraisingly. "Richie thinks you come outta the motel deal smellin' like a rose when you had every chance to come out of it smellin' like the backside of the cowshed. Or smellin' like somethin' that meant good business for the undertaker." He paused just long enough to lend emphasis to the question that followed. "Richie's curious to know if you got somethin' on Harrington?"

It was entirely in character for a shrewd operator like Richie Hoey to sense the ground swell before the first waves appeared. And to send an emissary to take soundings. "Harrington's not as young as he used to be, Sam." I fenced.

Carstens' level stare revealed nothing of his inner thoughts. "Nobody seen no indication of him applyin' for retirement heretofore, Wilson."

"He had an operation recently, too."

"We know about the operation. I'll put it to you plain, Wilson. Was this a one-shot deal, with you gettin' out from under a personal load, or are you makin' a move? You don't need to answer me, but it couldn't hurt you with Richie was you to give him an idea."

I checked the reply I had ready. If Richie Hoey was opposed to my making a move, Carstens wouldn't have appeared in my back yard. Not as a smoker of peace pipes, anyway. If Hoey and others like him weren't opposed to a move against Harrington, I might be able to move a lot faster than I'd dreamed possible. And hard on the heels of that thought came the realization of how I could move fastest of all. I made up my mind. "I'm taking over, Sam," I said flatly.

He nodded. "Richie kind of thought you might have it in mind." There was no expression in his tone. "That's why I'm here, because Richie's not choosin' up sides. He's worked with Tom Harrington a long time, but Richie's a businessman. If Harrington's through, Richie 'd like to see you 'n him do business along the same general lines. *If* Harrington's through."

"He's through."

"I hear you sayin' so."

"I'm still walking around, Sam."

"People do be wonderin' 'bout that," Carstens admitted. "What you got in mind, Wilson? Partic'larly?"

"For Harrington?"

"For you."

I'd never met Richie Hoey, but I knew his reputation. He wasn't an easy man to impress, but if I impressed him sufficiently, it could keep him from coming to Harrington's aid in the squeeze play that was bound to follow. "I think Harrington's a piker, Sam," I said.

Still his expression didn't change. "He done piked his way along for a right smart number of years."

I hit him with the second barrel. "I'm marrying Ludmilla Pierson, Sam."

Sam Carstens was not an easy man to impress, either, but that one really fetched him. His eyes widened, then narrowed, while his thin lips pursed in a soundless whistle. Twice he started to speak, and twice he stopped. "Reckon ol' Richie knew what he was doin' when he aimed me this way this evenin'," he finally said drily. "He'll be right interested in hearin' that. Right interested. Gonna be soon?"

"As soon as we figure the noise won't blow the roof off."

His grin was wry. "See what you mean. An' then?"

"Business as usual. Ludmilla would like to have Richie and a few of his friends over for dinner some evening soon after the wedding."

Carstens nodded slowly. "You got the program, man. No doubt about it." He hesitated. "If—"

"If my foot doesn't slip? Tell Richie not to worry about it. I've been getting ready for five years."

"I reckon," Carstens said. "D'you think—"

"I've heard a lot of nice things about the job you're doing for Richie, Sam," I interrupted. "And I need a reliable man in your end of the state. Contacts, that sort of thing. Is there any way I could persuade you to go to work for me?"

The usual mask was back in place on his face. "Richie's been right fair with me, Wilson."

"If you say so," I agreed. "The offer's open, though."

"Appreciate it," Carstens said, closing the subject. I

didn't especially want to hire him, although he'd have been a handy type to have available. I knew he'd report the offer to Richie, though, if only to prove that a prophet was without honor in his own country, and this gesture, more than any declaration of mine, would convince Richie I meant business. "Can you think of anything else in the line of news I should carry back to Richie?" Carstens continued.

"You don't think you've got enough now to hold him for a while?"

He grinned. "Could be I do, at that."

"You might tell Richie not to expect Harrington to drop out of sight completely. Not right away. People are used to working with him, so why upset things by changing the look of the whole face of nature? If someone else is pulling the strings, there's no need to let the world know about it."

"Richie appreciates that kind of thinkin'," Carstens said. "Business as usual, that's his motto. Well"—he rose to his feet—"thanks for the steak. An' the talk. I'll just mosey out the way I come in. No need for you to walk out with me."

"Tell Richie he's going to like the setup."

"He'll let you know fast enough if he don't." Carstens went down the walk unhurriedly. In seconds I heard the p-p-ping of the closing gate, and a moment later the sound of a car starting up.

I brushed the remains of our steak dinners to one side and rested my elbows on the formica table top. On balance, the unexpected confrontation had gone well. I had impressed Carstens. His whole attitude had changed after the revelation about Ludmilla. In a different way, Richie Hoey's reaction was bound to be the same. And if Harrington tried any smart moves now, before I was ready to oust him altogether, this should spike his guns. I couldn't see how Richie Hoey would choose up sides against me now. And Richie could be depended upon to get the word around where it would do the most good.

There was still a question in my mind whether the percentage gain counterbalanced my hundred-and-eighty-degree swing around to embracing the idea of marrying Lud Pierson.

It better had, though. It damn well better had because it was the only aspect of the forthcoming nuptials I could swallow without choking.

CHAPTER VII

A MONTH SLIPPED BY, a month of sixteen-hour workdays. We had a lot to do: hire more men; enlarge the bituminous batching plant to take care of the increased quantities necessary for a job of that size; clean up all the equipment for the changeover from concrete to bituminous; stockpile sand and gravel, since the pits were at a distance; and accumulate quantities of two-and-a-half-inch stone for the roadbed's binder course and three-eighths-inch stone for its wearing course.

I was working hard but enjoying it. Before, I'd always felt frustrated by the small jobs that had come our way, with their consequent lack of opportunity to make full use of what I liked to think was my organizational ability. And most of the time I'd been so busy scrounging around for an additional few dollars to keep us going that it had been difficult to take any real pleasure in the work. I had no problem like that now. Lud had been as good as her word in setting up a financial connection for me after I told her the marriage was on. It was a strange feeling to walk into a bank just twenty-five miles away and be addressed as "Mr. Wilson."

I had plenty of opportunity now for detailed planning. On day-to-day performance, Wing was great, but he was constitutionally unable to see beyond sunset of a given day. Long ago I'd learned to give him performance sheets to keep him on the rails. With a sheet to guide him, he'd keep a crew out on the job site until midnight, if necessary, to finish a specific assignment. And they'd work for him, where they wouldn't have for me.

Wing would gather the whole crew around him in the

morning, sheet in hand. "Today we grade an' level the next section, boys. Sand it, gravel it, stone it, an' pour an' roll at least the breakin'-down pass," he'd say. "An' we don't go home 'til we've done it." If they finished an hour early, he let them go an hour early. It wasn't the way I'd have handled it, but it worked for him, and I kept my nose out of that end of it.

He called me at the house on a hot Saturday afternoon. "C'mon out to the cabin, hoss," he said. "I got some stuff out here."

His voice slurred, indicating an early start on the weekend's drinking. I knew what his "stuff" would be: in addition to that in bottles, it would be seventeen years old, platinumed, and already two years experienced. I didn't want to go, but I hesitated to say "No" for two reasons. The first was that I wanted to reestablish the rapport with Wing we'd had formerly. A refusal on the first real social gesture he'd made in weeks was hardly the way to begin bridging the chasm.

The second reason was even more important. I couldn't wait any longer to tell him I was going to marry Lud Pierson. I wanted him to hear it from me before he had even a hint from anyone else. I'd purposely held off on the house calls Lud wanted me to make until I could find a way to break the news to Wing. In a town like Moline, there was bound to be active speculation as soon as I began making the calls. Public opinion in general, I didn't give a damn about, any more than Ludmilla did; but there were a couple of areas that needed more careful handling, and Wing Darlington was one of them.

"I'll be out in an hour," I promised.

"Great, man. Bring hormones," he said. Then he hung up.

I used most of the hour to finish up a wad of paperwork, then drove out to the cabin. The only surprise there was that my seventeen-year-old had black hair instead of silvery blonde. "Gracie an' Dolly," Wing said, introducing them. "This heah is Jim, girls." Mine was Dolly, a plump, olive-skinned girl looking more than a little nervous. Wing's was the usual platinumed job, taller and more slender—Wing liked the greyhound type—with slightly buck teeth distracting from better than average features. In contrast to her friend, Gracie seemed completely at her ease.

Wing handed around a tray of drinks, and I spent the next thirty minutes catching up in that department. There's nothing worse than a party at which you're more sober than everyone else. By the time I felt adjusted, the four of us were on the bed in the large bedroom. "Interestin' differential in the color specifications between this heah area an' your topknot," Wing informed Gracie.

"You quit that!" she yelped. "You hear me? You—oh!"

Wing scooped her up abruptly and marched to the door leading to the other bedroom. When I turned my head Dolly's eyes were on the gun rack in the corner, on which Wing kept his deer rifle. From the expression on her face, I thought it just as well she didn't know there were half a dozen hand guns in the cabinet behind it.

"Afraid of me?" I asked her.

"N-no," she said uncertainly.

I let the dialogue expire. Dolly wasn't much good in harness; at that age they never are. We were taking ten when we heard a patter of bare feet, and Gracie trotted in from the other bedroom. She was in her pelt, and she laughed at Dolly's scrambling efforts to hide her own exposure. Wing came in from the kitchen in a state of nature, carrying a tray of drinks. When we finished them, I took the tray back for refills. After a while I took Gracie into the smaller bedroom. She was eager, if inexpert. When we returned, Wing was sitting on the edge of the bed beside a bemused-looking Dolly. "You really got a yard of ass, honey," he was saying to the plump girl. "Some one of these days you're gonna make a damn fine little mare when you get settled in proper to a stud."

We took time out for a chicken fry with Wing officiating —neither of the girls could boil water—and a load of beer, then readjourned to the bedrooms. The girls had quit on the hard stuff, but Wing went drink for drink with me. He's tried it a few times, with mixed results, but at midnight he was still bright-eyed and bushy-tailed. The girls were in the shower and Wing and I were on the big bed, smoking. "Like old times, huh, hoss?" Wing said lazily.

"Yes. Wing?"

"Yeah?"

I didn't know how to begin. He rolled over to look at me inquiringly. "I'm marrying Ludmilla Pierson," I said at last. "Soon."

He laughed. "You turnin' comedian on me now, ol' salty dog?"

"I'm serious, Wing."

He shook his head, smiling good-humoredly. "You better get you a new gag writer."

"It makes sense, Wing. When you think about it. She can do us a lot of good. She has connections we can't touch otherwise. We'd never have another worry about financing. We could be the biggest outfit in the state. Hell, there'd be something the matter with us if we weren't the biggest."

His smile had gradually disappeared, and he was regarding me with a puzzled expression. "You're serious? I mean you think you're goin' to marry Lud?" He laughed again, but not as loudly as before. "The way you two feel about each other?"

"Wing, I'm going to marry her."

"You done stripped your gears, man," he said positively. "Not to rub yore nose in it, but she'd use your balls for emery paper did she get the chance."

"She's practical, Wing. As practical as I am. She wants to run things, but she needs a man to do it. She's—"

" 'Pears to me the idea of runnin' things has got to *you*, not her, friend. The way you been actin' lately an' all. You're all the time sayin' think big, but the day you think big enough to imagine all you got to do is ask Ludmilla Pierson to marry you an' you got it made around these parts—"

"Wing."

99

He stopped.

"It's settled. She's marrying me."

Something changed in his eyes; I couldn't decide what it was. "You never lied to me yet, hoss," he said after a pause.

"And I'm not lying to you now. Can't you see that it makes sense? Can't you see what it could mean for both of us? We could have things—"

"She's said she's marryin' you?" he interrupted. "She's said so in so many words?"

"It's signed, sealed, and all but delivered."

He was silent for a full ten seconds. "Hoss, you're just a natural-born loser," he said at last. "Why don't you—oh, Christ, the hell with it. You an' your power complex."

His bitterness surprised me. "The important thing is it's a shortcut to everything we've—hey, what's the matter?"

He had bounded from the bed, a dark flush of anger staining his bronzed features. "Do I call you Mr. Wilson now?" he inquired sarcastically. Then he stalked from the room.

In seconds, I heard a sharp crack and Gracie's startled exclamation. "*Owww*! What was *that* for?"

"Git yore ass into yore clothes." I hardly recognized Wing's voice. "We're leavin'."

I got off the bed and went into the hall and down it to the shower. The area was crowded with naked bodies. "What are you so upset about, Wing? It's not going to make any difference to us, for God's sake. You've seen me use people before when it was to our advantage, haven't you?"

He refused to look at me. "Get dressed," he snapped at Gracie. "Less'n you want to ride home in yore skin."

She ran past me. Dolly followed more slowly, turning to look back at us. I was still trying to guess the reason for Wing's anger. "You don't think I'm turning my back on the partnership? That's the last—"

He pushed past me without a word, following the girls into the large bedroom. After a moment, I went into the kitchen, opened a bottle of beer, and carried it in to

100

Dolly. She accepted it absentmindedly. Her eyes were on Gracie, half-dressed, and Wing, who was already into his pants. The plump girl set the bottle down abruptly. "I'm going, too," she announced. "I don't want to be left—" She didn't finish it. She scrambled to her feet and began pulling her dress on over her head.

I made one more try at Wing. "When have I ever steered you wrong, man? I tell you this is the way to do it. What are you getting so hot about? I'm not turning my back on my old friends just because of what this can mean. You know me better than that. You know—"

His expression was like an Indian's. "I used to think I knew you—" He bit off and charged toward the door. Gracie followed him, looking back at me curiously. Dolly ran after them, carrying her shoes and underwear in one hand. In seconds, I heard the spatter of gravel against the cabin wall and the roar of Wing's car as he gunned it out of the parking slot into the driveway and out onto the highway. I could hear the squeal of his tires as he accelerated.

I stood for a moment in the bedroom; it had suddenly become quiet. I could hear water dripping in the shower, and I walked down to it and turned the faucets off, hard, then looked at the imprint of the metal in my palm.

Why was Wing so upset? Because he felt he was being deliberately relegated to a position as a minor cog on the wheel? Somehow I was going to have to get through to him that nothing had really changed between us.

I gave it up, went into the kitchen, opened up a fresh bottle of bourbon, and drank myself blind.

I woke late Sunday afternoon with my mouth tasting like a mildewed rubber boot. I stumbled in and out of the shower, then took a quick tour of the cabin. The kitchen was a mess; empty bottles and glasses were everywhere. I'd neglected to open a window, and the air was heavy with the odor of perspiration, chicken grease, and stale beer. I left everything just as it was and drove home. I'd send a cleaning woman out tomorrow.

By the time I reached the house my head was throbbing so fiercely I knew I had to have a drink. I had my hand on the gin bottle on the top shelf in the kitchen when the telephone rang. I debated not answering it, but on the chance it was Wing, I walked into the front hall. "Yes?" I said. I hardly recognized my own voice.

"Jim? Oh, Jim, where h-have you *been*! I've been t-trying to reach you for two wh-whole *days*!" It was Veronica, and she sounded almost hysterical. She burst into noisy tears and talked so fast between sobs that my splitting head couldn't absorb what she was trying to tell me.

"Whoa, whoa," I interrupted. "Take it slower. What's it all about?"

"Mr. Cartwright c-caught me s-searching his private file yesterday," she sniffled. "And he—he *f-fired* me. And a f-friend just called me from city h-hall and s-said two detectives were c-coming here to ar-rest me!" Her voice trailed off in a wail.

"Arrest you? For what, for God's sake?" But even as I said it, I knew. Not arrest her; not really. Just take her in on a Sunday night when she couldn't reach anyone, throw the fear of God into her, and release her quietly on Monday morning. It was a tactic that had Tom Harrington's thumbprint all over it.

"Jim, what am I g-going to *do*?" she whimpered. "They're on their way n-now. I thought I'd *n-never* reach you."

It was difficult to think with my head clanging like dull iron, but on the other hand, there wasn't much to think about. I couldn't afford to let this happen. Harrington's response was aimed at least as much at me as it was at Veronica, and if I couldn't protect anyone associated with me, I was in a bad way. "Don't open the door," I said at last. "Understand? Don't open it." They wouldn't have a warrant, and I didn't think they'd risk forcing the door. They'd try to bull her into going quietly with them.

"H-how can I k-keep them out?" She was crying openly again.

"Keep it locked," I said impatiently. "If they sound nasty, tell them you have a gun and will use it."

"Jim, you're coming over h-here? P-please?"

"I'm coming. But remember, just sit tight. Don't let anyone in until you hear from me. *Anyone*."

"*Please* h-hurry," she said. She was sobbing as I hung up the phone.

I drove directly to Tom Harrington's big place on Jackson Street. It wouldn't be the first time Chet Dorsey's boys had unofficially roughed up someone who had incurred Tom Harrington's displeasure. Harrington had given the order, I was positive, and he could countermand it. His Cadillac was in the garage, so I wasn't too concerned when half a dozen rings of his doorbell produced no action. I went down the front steps to his driveway, found a good-sized rock, went back up the steps, and threw the rock through the front door glass, which disappeared in a welter of smashing crystal particles. I reached inside and unlocked the door.

I'd been in the house often enough with Mona, and I walked to Harrington's study. The door was closed, and I opened it without knocking. Tom Harrington sat at his old-fashioned rolltop desk with his white head cocked to one side above an ancient .44 in his right hand. Its barrel was half as long as a .30-.30. The .44 was poised negligently, aimed halfway between the door and me. "I got ev'ry right in the world to cut loose on you, Wilson," Harrington said harshly. "Bustin' into my house like this."

"If you were going to do it, you wouldn't be talking about it," I said. I didn't make any sudden moves, though. I could see a bullet in each chamber of the rickety-looking old gun; whether there was one under the hammer I couldn't tell, and I wasn't fussy about finding out. At that distance, even a peashooter carries a sting. "There's no need to get excited. Just cut the crap and call your dogs off Veronica Peters."

His yellow-flecked eyes examined me. "She hung her own ass out on the line, sonny. She can wear what she gets."

"If she has to wear anything, you won't enjoy the after-math, you hear me?" Almost carelessly, the .44 lined itself up on my head. "I s'pose you're tellin' me you'll close my balls up in my own desk drawer, like you did with Fred Hunter a few years back?"

Moving with slow deliberation, I slid a straight-backed chair into position across from Harrington's worn swivel chair and sat down in it. I slid it because picking it up could have been a mistake. "I'm marrying Lud Pierson, Harrington," I said slowly and distinctly. "Next month. If you don't believe me, pick up the phone and ask her."

Harrington was an old man who hadn't too much starch left to begin with or I'd never have got that far inside his study, but I could see whatever he had left oozing out of him. He'd been around a long time, and he didn't need to be kicked by a mule's rear heels to know that they were loaded. Head-to-head, he might have had a chance still to upset a young upstart like me; with Lud on my team he didn't have a prayer, and he knew it. I was counting most on the fact that a man in his position should be asking himself if, after all the years of scrambling, it was worthwhile to go down with the ship.

" 'Pears like you're playin' right handy cards, Wilson, if you don't find a joker in the deck," he said at last. His voice was cracked.

The .44 had moved only three inches out of line with my head, but it had moved. Moving slowly and easily, I leaned forward and picked up the telephone on his desk. His yellow-tinged eyes never looked away from me as I dialed. "Veronica? Jim. This is what I want you to do. Go to the door—"

"Oh, Jim! Two men have been knocking on the door for ten minutes! What am I going to do? They keep it up and *keep* it up. I'm—"

"Shut up and listen, will you? And do what I tell you. Go to the door and call out to them that there's a tele-phone call for them on your line. Then before you unlock the door and remove the chain latch, push every chair in the place over in front of the door. While they're pushing their way in past the chairs, you run into the bathroom and lock yourself in. Have you got that?"

"I th-thought you were coming here, Jim? I—I can't unlock that door. I'm *afraid*. They'll—they'll—"

"Do as I tell you, damn it! Right now!"

For an instant, the sound of her sobbing breath hung in my ear; then it was gone. I could have counted to three hundred while faint, unidentifiable noises emanated from the receiver. Then there was a scrabbling sound and a harsh voice in my ear. "Garvey," it said.

I handed the phone to Harrington. "Who is it?" he asked after clearing his throat.

"Frank Garvey," I could hear Garvey repeat.

"This is Harrington. Pack up and get out of there, Garvey. I've changed my mind."

There was a pause. "But Chet said—"

"To hell with what Chet said!" For an instant, the old snarl was back in Harrington's voice. "I said I've changed my mind!"

There was another pause. Frank Garvey was a shrewd, tough-minded individual who wore no man's collar and had never advanced far in the department because of it. I knew he was mentally reviewing the conversation to decide if there had been a personal affront. "It's your mind," he said laconically at last. "It does seem you'd know it better. Anything else?"

"Nothing," Harrington said. He cradled the receiver without looking at me.

Sometime during the conversation, the .44 had disappeared. I got to my feet. "Thanks for the cooperation, Harrington," I said as I moved toward the door.

His lips came back from his teeth, but he didn't say anything.

I went outside to the station wagon and drove to Veronica's. Across the street from her apartment building, Frank Garvey was seated in his car, alone. Naturally, Garvey would have waited to see who'd put the chain on the dog. I walked across the street to his car. He looked up at me. "You ought to get with a winner," I told him.

"Seems like it might not be a bad idea, after today," he agreed.

I glanced up at the windows of Veronica's apartment. "What was the word that went with the package?"

"Rough it up 'til it hollered. Nothin' she couldn't have lived with afterward."

"Fine work for a grown man, Garvey."

He shook his head. "You ain't needlin' me out've this car, Wilson. An' if I do got to come out, I come out shootin', understand? You ain't workin' off no head of steam on this mother's son."

I changed horses in midstream. "On getting with a winner, why don't you drop around to the back door some night and we'll talk things over?"

"When I make up my mind about you, Wilson, I'll meet you at high noon on Main Street an' talk to you. I ain't hidin' from no one."

"What is there to make up your mind about?"

He squinted up at me. "When a guy like you goes down, Wilson, he takes a lot of people with him. Innocent bystanders, some of 'em like the kid upstairs. I ain't innocent or exactly a bystander, either, an' I got to like your chances a little bit better'n what I do right now."

"Don't miss the boat," I warned him. Then I walked back across the street. Going up in the self-service elevator, I thought about Garvey. I could use him, or someone like him. For weeks now, I'd had the feeling that things had speeded up too much, that they were moving too fast, that there were no longer enough hours in the day. I was so busy on the Edmonds Road job that I didn't have time for other things, important things that needed doing, like finding out who'd tampered with George Pierson's car. Once, I'd had Wing for jobs like that. Now I considered myself lucky that he was still out on the job every day.

I had to knock for a good three minutes before Veronica opened the door just a crack on the chain latch. When she saw who it was, she fumbled the door wide open and collapsed into my arms, crying and shivering and shaking. Two days of tears had left her eyes red-rimmed,

106

and her usually pleasant features looked both puffy and drawn. "Oh, J-Jim!" she choked, holding onto to me tightly. "Oh, J-Jim!"

She was almost in a state of shock; the flesh of her arms was chilly to the touch. After closing and locking the door again, I maneuvered her into her bedroom and began getting her out of her clothes. She looked as if she'd slept in them. She seemed to need physical reassurance; every time I removed one of the hands clutching at me, another took its place. I went to her bureau and routed out a nightgown, finished undressing her, and got her into it. Her big, womanly body appeared shrunken, somehow.

I found a hairbrush in the bathroom and brushed out her hair—it looked like wild Aggie's. She sat docilely on the side of the bed. Every time I got up—once for a wet towel to wash her face; once for drops for her swollen eyes—she tried to restrain me with a hand on my arm. When I had her looking semirespectable again, I motioned her to the bed. "Stretch out," I told her. "Relax. You're still tighter than a vestal virgin."

She eased herself down with a tired sigh. "My stomach hurts," she said forlornly.

"That's from tension."

"Sit with me," she pleaded when I started to clean up some of the debris in the bedroom. I sat down with her again. She was crying quietly, big round tears that slid slowly down her cheeks. "You'll n-never s-speak to me again for being s-such a baby," she sobbed.

I knew why she'd been so frantic. Four years ago, a tall, good-looking girl named Jessie Stanley had fallen in love with one of Roy Hargrave's kid reporters. Jessie was working in Tom Harrington's office, and she leaked a story on a contract to her boy friend. The *Clarion* had used the story, and Harrington had blown his stack. He ran the kid reporter out of town for a starter, and then the word went around among the insiders that four of Chet's boys had taken Jessie down into the basement of the jail and whipped her tail with a trunk strap. Hargraves chickened out on backing her up afterward, she couldn't get another job locally, and she'd left town and gone to Charleston. Eighteen months ago, when I'd first begun looking for an angle on Harrington, I'd driven over to Charleston, looked her up, and made her a proposition. She'd heard me out, then shook her head. "It might work, Jim, but I haven't the nerve for it. Not after—after—try me again in another year." In another year I'd had plans that didn't include Jessie Stanley but I still remembered her eyes. She hadn't been over it then.

"You'll hate me for being s-such a s-sissy," Veronica was moaning.

"Don't talk foolishly," I said. I was somewhere between a feeling of pity for her and a feeling of impatience with her. She was at least half right; I'd grown up with girls who in her situation would have bared it to the strap and not only looked the whole town in the eye afterward but had the strap swingers watching where they put their feet down on dark nights. On the other hand Veronica couldn't change her own nature.

"Hold my hand," she whispered.

I held her hand. Sitting there, listening to the ragged edge leave her breathing, I felt the toll of my own weekend. Twice I felt my eyes closing. I stopped fighting it, finally. I kicked off my shoes, took off my shirt, and stretched out beside Veronica. She put her arms around me at once. She still wanted to talk. To explain herself. "Hush," I said when she started to say something, and it was the last thing I remembered for a while.

When I opened my eyes again, it was almost dark. A single lamp was on in the bedroom, and Veronica was floating around in a fresh nightie. She appeared normal except for her reddened eyes. Evidently she'd put some time on her face at the boudoir mirror. She saw me watching her and came over to the bed smiling kittenishly. Great, I thought. She felt kittenish; I didn't. I spoke before she could. "I've been screwing all weekend, Veronica, and I've got to get back to the house and get things sorted out."

He smile froze grotesquely. "Oh," she said weakly. For

108

once the English language seemed to have dried up on her.

I got up from her bed. "Do you want to go back to the office in the morning?"

She stared at me, unable, for an instant, to make the transition. "Do I want—you mean the Cartwright office? I can't. Mr. Cartwright f-fired me." Quick tears of self-pity filled her eyes.

"He'll unfire you if you want to go back."

"Well," she said uncertainly. "I'm not—I don't—it's a good job."

I went to her telephone and dialed Cartwright's house. "Wilson, Vic. Veronica will be in at the usual time in the morning."

He'd already had the word but he was prepared to argue. "I don't think it's wise, Jim. There can only be embarrassment on both sides. Another arrangement—"

"You just heard the arrangement. And if I get any echoes I don't like, it won't be Veronica who's embarrassed. Understand?"

His tone changed to one of resignation. "I'll be expecting her, then."

"No problem," I said to Veronica as I hung up the phone. I walked to the door and she followed me out into the hall. "I'll call you," I added as an afterthought. I was almost out the door before I remembered what all the shooting had been about. I turned back to her. "What did you find in the file?"

"Nothing worth all the trouble I got into," she said resentfully. "All that Mr. Cartwright's notes said were that he was trying to get a statement from a man named Roger Manton, who didn't want to make one."

Roger Manton had driven the dead blackmailer from Spartanburg to Moline. Had in fact driven him to my back door. I'd traced Manton's name through the license number of his car as he circled the block waiting for his partner, who never reappeared. It seemed I was going to have to take a trip to Spartanburg. Although with no body, what could they do?

"I'll call you," I repeated to Veronica. She seemed

to be waiting to hear something else, but I had nothing else to say. I went out the door.

It was probably true, I reflected as I walked down the hall. Almost certainly I would call her again. She was good in bed, she was available, and now she was under obligation.

But somehow, after seeing her go to pieces like that, I knew it was never going to be as good again.

CHAPTER VIII

LUD AND I were married by a Justice of the Peace at five-thirty on a Friday afternoon, and we left immediately for a long weekend at Nags Head, where Lud had a cottage. There had been no preliminary announcement of the wedding, and the JP and his wife were the only witnesses. Lud wore a pastel blue, knee-length dress with three-quarter-length sleeves; and I had on my only business suit. During the drive to the coast, Lud wasn't exactly bursting with song, but she looked as satisfied as any other woman getting her own way.

We stopped to eat around eight o'clock, and it was a strange sort of wedding feast. We both had steak, medium-rare, with french fries and string beans, coffee, and no dessert. I hoped the utilitarian meat-and-potatoes meal was an omen for the marriage, but I doubted it.

It was a long drive to the cottage, and we didn't arrive until a few minutes before midnight. When I got out of the car, I could smell the salt in the sea breeze and hear the sound of nearby surf. The air was almost chilly. I carried our bags inside while Lud went from room to room switching on lights. The bedroom to which she directed me had only one bed in it, a monstrous affair that could have slept six people comfortably. I arranged our bags on folding racks and went back out into the living room.

"A nightcap?" Lud asked brightly. There was a luster about her, not soft and glowing, but hard and shiny. "The liquor's in the cabinet there." She indicated a walnut console in one corner that could have housed a Volkswagen. She produced a key from her handbag and held it out to me.

I shook my head. "I'm ready for bed," I said.

"I'm tired, too," she agreed at once. "You use the bathroom first, Jim. It will take me longer."

I used the bathroom first, then crawled into the enormous bed and turned on my side with my back to the boudoir light that was the room's only illumination. For what seemed like hours, I could hear Lud's slithering bedroom-slippered progress back and forth between her bags and the bathroom. I was legitimately tired, but I forced myself to stay awake. I wanted to be awake when she finally came to bed.

When the springs creaked at last, announcing her arrival, I raised my voice. "Good night," I said.

"Good night," she replied after a five second pause.

Before I fell asleep, I felt her make several cautious readjustments in her position and move close enough to me so that I could feel her body heat; but she was never quite touching me.

Then I went under completely.

I woke in the gray light of dawn, on my back, staring up at the ceiling of a strange room. I glanced at the adjoining pillow and the sense of disorientation lasted a second longer because Lud was sleeping with an arm over her eyes and the usually firm line of her jaw was so softened in sleep that I hardly recognized her. She was half out of the sheet that was our only covering, and the portion of her nightgown visible to me appeared to consist principally of lace. Porous lace. I eased out of bed without waking her, found a pair of swim trunks in my bag, and let myself out the kitchen door.

The air outside was cold and damp, with feathers of fog blowing about. I followed a steep path two hundred yards down to a sand beach where three foot rollers crashed steadily. I tested the water with a toe. It was nippy, but not as much so as the air. I waded into a breaking wave, paddled my way out beyond the surf,

111

and floated about for a few minutes. When the chill began to get to me, I rode a wave back in.

Walking back up to the cottage, I realized for the first time how isolated it was. Although we had passed other cottages on the way in the previous night, I couldn't see any of them. Ten yards from the kitchen door there was an outside shower connected to a water tank, and I stripped off my trunks and stepped under it to sluice the salt water off me. The water of the shower was chillier than that of the ocean. From the corner of my eye I caught a flash of pink at a kitchen window. When I went back inside, though, the kitchen was quiet and Lud was in bed, presumably asleep.

I went into the bathroom and shaved, and when I came out, Lud still hadn't moved in the bed. I went into the kitchen and opened the refrigerator and examined its well-stocked contents. I put on the coffee, slung together a mess of bacon and eggs, dropped bread in the toaster, and found a large tray. I filled it with bacon-and-egg-laden plates, cups and saucers, cutlery, buttered toast, jelly, and a coffeepot. I carried the tray into the bedroom. "Breakfast," I announced.

"Mmmmph," Lud said, apparently from the depths of slumber. The one eye she opened was suspiciously bright, though. She stretched enthusiastically, straining the froth of lace encompassing her pear-shaped breasts. She bounded from bed energetically. "Got to wash my filthy face," she announced as she went past me, her long legs scissoring beneath the gossamer transparency of her gown. She returned in a moment and propped herself up against doubled-up pillows while I placed the tray on her knees. I pulled up a chair and poured the coffee; we ate heartily. Lud sank back with her hands folded over the bowl of her stomach when I removed the tray. "I see your trunks are wet," she said. "I must take a dip, too. How's the water?"

"Cool. No newspapers out here, I suppose?"

"Only on Sunday. And no television. There's a radio in the living room."

I went in to turn it on and try to catch the news. In a

few minutes, Lud emerged from the bedroom in a two-piece bathing suit that was so skimpy it covered perhaps a twelfth of her. "You're not afraid of cramps?" I asked her. "After that meal?"

"I'm not going to swim," she replied. "I'm just going to get wet. I'll be back in a few minutes."

I had turned off the radio and was out in the kitchen doing up the breakfast dishes when she came up the path from the beach. After a quick glance toward the house, she peeled off her suit and stepped under the open shower. The cold water surprised her; she skipped sideways involuntarily, then inched back beneath it cautiously. Seen back to, she had a beautifully even tan, with the exception of a narrow band of flesh marking the bra strap of her swim suit, plus a not-much-wider splash of white across her buttocks, which were slim and springy-looking, not quite boyish, but with no customary feminine amplitude. Swathing herself in a huge towel, she walked into the kitchen. "Your domesticity amazes me," she remarked, with a side glance at me in front of the sink, before she disappeared into the bedroom with an artful slippage of her towel that disclosed a single glistening haunch.

The farce continued all day. We didn't go anywhere, and we didn't do anything but eat, yet she changed her clothes four times, each time with a studied casualness that still contrived to reveal an ensemble of flesh that would have brought Simeon Stylites down from his pillar. Or me, except that I had turned my motor off.

I was first into bed again that night, and when the bed creaked under her weight, I spoke my piece. "Good night," I said.

There was a long silence. "Jim," she said finally. I rolled over to look at her. She was kneeling straight up on the edge of the bed, and she had dispensed with the lace. "I want a husband, Jim. Can I put it more plainly?"

"You can, and I have no doubt you will, but that's beside the point. You don't have a husband. You have a business partner."

"There's no reason we can't get along," she said coaxingly.

"We will get along, but not in bed."

"But why? Will you please tell me why?"

"Because I'm all through letting women like you emasculate me. That's why."

She started to bend down over me, then reconsidered. "Once and for all, Jim, I'm not like that. Can't you understand? I'm simply not like that. Mona and I in college—that doesn't count, Jim. Where were the men? And I was merely the one she returned to when her crushes broke up, anyway." She was choosing her words carefully. "There's more than one kind of pleasure in the world, you know. Let's face it. Mona didn't have much fun. You can argue 'til you're blue in the face whether it was her fault or not, but the fact remains that she *didn't* have much fun. When she kept after me to return to—to—well, sometimes I accomodated her. What did it cost me? But what you're accusing me of—no."

"I don't believe you, Lud. Mona was all right when I married her."

"Mona was never all right, and one of these days you'll admit it. I couldn't believe it when you married her. *You*, of all people. I could understand why she did it easily enough—it represented one last try at escaping from herself. I *liked* Mona, but as a man's wife—" She didn't finish.

"How did you get sucked into that movie deal?"

She was silent for a moment. "I suppose that's the thing you're never going to forgive," she said at last. "There were four women partying in a cabin up at the lake, and we kept egging each other on. What I didn't realize was that the partying had been going on all summer with different groups, and the cabin had a reputation. Sometime during the week, when no one was there, that sonofabitch of a blackmailer bored a hole in the outside wall for his camera lens, and there we were. I think I'd have killed him myself if I'd been alone when he first approached me. But he was too smart for that; he walked up to me on the street in broad daylight, and I had to smile sweetly and pretend everything was all

114

right." Her voice changed. "He must have given you a far better opportunity."

"When I bought the film from him, you mean?" I said.

"That's not what I mean. You—"

I rolled away from her again. "Good night, Lud."

She placed a hand on my shoulder. "I can prove every word I've said to you just now, but not by myself."

I spoke to the wall. "I don't want you, Lud. Do I have to take an ad in the *Clarion*?"

She snatched her hand away. "You damned prig! I had better men than you before I was fifteen!"

"Then go round up a few. You obviously don't need me."

She flounced angrily from the bed, and I must have been asleep when she returned because I didn't hear her.

She sulked all the next morning while I read the Sunday paper, but in the afternoon she snapped out of it far enough to prove to me that she hadn't taken her eye off the main chance. She went out to the car and took a heavy briefcase from its trunk. When I saw what she was doing, I set up two card tables in the living room. She sat down across from me at one table, put on her glasses, and began unloading the briefcase. "Do you know what your biggest problem is going to be in Moline now?" she asked. Her tone was strictly business.

"What's that?"

"You've always been the underdog around town before now, and despite certain tactics you've employed, that fact has earned you a certain amount of sympathy. That won't hold true any longer. In the eyes of the townspeople, you've crossed over from the have-nots to the haves."

"I don't see any problem."

"You can't expect the same laissez-faire attitude in the future toward your strong-arm methods. People will resent it. You're going to have to change your approach."

"I'll worry about it when I run into it."

She shrugged. "Hardheaded. All right. See what you think of this."

She handed me the top paper on the pile, and for four hours we went through the contents of the briefcase. At the end of this period I found myself admiring Ludmilla Pierson-Wilson more than I would have thought possible. She had both a sharp eye for a column of figures and a pragmatic ability at character assessment. We talked over people and situations on the most realistic level, and not once could I fault her judgement. "And I thought I was hard-boiled," I said finally.

"Take a look at this," was her only reply. She laid out on the table what proved to be the master plan in a step-by-step campaign by which we would be able to take over control in the state. Phase One was so detailed and so thoroughly documented I could only shake my head. Another hour's discussion and we had hammered the occasional rough spot out of it.

At the conference table we got on well, but we went to bed that night without a word being spoken on either side.

Monday we put in another session at the card tables.

"I'd intended to begin socially with a number of small dinner parties," Lud started off that morning. "As per these lists. Just for the people that matter; not in Moline, but from around the state. But now I believe that one large dinner is a better idea as an entering wedge; have them all in at once to absorb the atmosphere of the change. How about two weeks from Saturday?"

"Fine with me."

"We'll invite Tom Harrington."

I looked at her. She was looking down at her lists. "What the hell's new about that?"

She took off her glasses to examine me. "I'd have thought your roughneck activities would have taught you never to push a man into a corner from which he can't retreat. That's when he's likely to do something desperate, not counting the cost. The people we invite will know that Harrington is harmless now, but he can still be useful as a showpiece."

Essentially it was the same thing I'd told Sam Carstens to carry back to Richie Hoey, but I didn't like it coming from Lud. I didn't say anything, though. I wanted to take a better look at my hole card before I started raising the pot.

She was watching my face. "Any objections?"

"When there are, you won't have to ask me."

"Good enough. Let's consolidate the major elements of these lists." She bent over the card table again and printed rapidly in a strong, square-looking script.

Tuesday morning we drove back to Moline. "Since we've arrived at a truce," she said to me as I was putting the bags in the trunk of the car, "let me tell you an essential condition of maintaining it. No tomcatting in Moline. I have my pride."

I turned halfway around to face her fully. "You can shove your pride, Lud. You're not running my private life. Not now and not ever. You've got a business arrangement, and that's all you've got."

She clouded up like a thunderstorm in the Rockies. "I won't have people thinking—"

"If it bothers you, hire a hall and we'll give them an exhibition"—I cut her off—"once. Just once."

She climbed into the car and slammed the door.

But five miles down the road she was speaking to me again, making further plans for the dinner party for Richie Hoey and the state's other wheelers and dealers.

That was the thing about Lud: business was business and it always came first. It was an attitude I appreciated.

CHAPTER IX

I KNEW I'd had it with Mona fifteen months before the end. I'd had more than my fill of suddenly averted glances and abrupt changes of conversation when I walked up to different groups in the country club locker room. The convincer, if I needed one, occurred when Wing and a couple of other good friends stopped coming to the house altogether. The cuckolded husband is always supposed to be the last to know. Sometimes it doesn't work that way.

It's one thing not to be making it with your wife, but it's another shade of red-winged blackbird to have her laying your friends and business acquaintances. Not because she wanted it but—as nearly as I was ever able to figure it out—for spite. It was never easy for me to try to talk to Mona because she'd been Mona Harrington and had a goddess complex that made communication with a peasant like me difficult for her. My own attempts seemed to irritate her, and interchange was at a low level.

We came in one evening from a dinner party, during which she'd been in a particularly foul mood, snapping peoples' heads off without provocation. It was in the spring of the year and the night temperatures were still in the fifties. It had been a nippy ride home in the bucket seats of the MG that was Mona's car that season. She would never ride in my car. Before we'd left home, I'd built a fire in the twelve-foot fireplace, and the oak log was still burning briskly when we returned. Mona went directly to the fireplace and stood back-to, to the fire with her skirt pulled up behind her, toasting the seat of her pants in an unconscious burlesque of the old print of a red-jacketed British rider-to-hounds warming himself by parting the tails of his jacket before a roaring fire.

I don't know why I picked that particular moment to bring things to a head. Certainly the evening had produced nothing new or unusual in her recent behavior pattern. It could have been that the ferment within me boiled up and took charge by itself. "Good show tonight," I said from the liquor cabinet, where I was pouring myself a drink. "I gave you four stars for bitchiness. Of course you could have done better if you'd been trying."

She stared at me suspiciously. Ordinarily I avoided head-on collisions with her. "Those stinking dinner parties," she said at last. "All that smug chitter-chatter simply infuriates me."

"This afternoon, too?" I said. "I didn't know Fred Wilkinson talked in bed."

Her expression hardened. It never occurred to her to take a backward verbal step. She was Mona Harrington. The fact that she was also Mona Wilson I had long since become convinced meant nothing to her. "If it's any comfort to your ego, dear, Fred's no better a performer than you are," she said bitingly. "Or any other of you insipid males."

I admired the steady hand with which I raised my glass to lower the level of its contents. "This insipid male wonders if you mightn't like a divorce, Mona?"

"Divorce?" she said sharply. "I should say not. What would I want with a divorce? I'd simply have to get another escort, wouldn't I?"

"There's that about it," I agreed. "But let's take it from a personal point of view. Mine, for a change. I've had it, Mona. I'm tired of having my wife referred to behind my back as the town pump. In fact, I'm through. _I_ want the divorce."

She laughed, a brittle sound. "You'll never get it," she stated positively. She moved away from the fire, releasing the skirt that had been bunched up around her waist, only to pick it up again immediately by its hem and draw it off over her head. Every time we had an argument, Mona took off her clothes. It seemed to be a compulsion with her. "You'll never get anyone to testify for you. My father will see to that. If you make just the first little move toward obtaining a divorce, he'll get rid of you like used toilet paper."

I tried to hold myself down. "You don't feel that the state of our marriage could be improved?"

"When I want it improved, I'll improve it," she snapped. "What are you complaining about?" She swept an arm around the comfortably furnished room. "You don't have it so bad. You get out of line, though, and you'll be digging ditches for the rest of your life." She was taking off her bra. "I like things the way they are, and that's the way they're going to stay."

"I'm trying to understand you," I said as she stepped out of her panties. She tossed them aside and went back to the fireplace and posed in front of the mantel.

119

"You egotistical fools!" she burst out. "I'll *never* understand what it is that gives any of you men a license to think he can satisfy a woman!"

"The operative word is 'woman,'" I said. "Basically, you like girls better than boys, Mona. Like Ludmilla Pierson. You—"

"You leave Ludmilla out of this!"

"Do you deny it?"

"My, how observant we are!" she jeered.

"How about going to a psychiatrist with me, Mona? I don't know if it would do any good, but it's just barely possible we might—"

I stopped. A dark red flush of anger had flooded her features. She left the fireplace, marched to where I was standing, and planted herself squarely in front of me, naked from her eyebrows to her stocking tops. "If I ever learn that you've been discussing me with a psychiatrist, Jim Wilson, it will be the sorriest day of your life. I'll live my own life and you'll keep your nose out of my affairs. It's none of your damn business what I do!" Her voice had turned both harsh and shrill.

"I'm married to you, and it's none of my business?"

"You heard me! If I take the notion, I'll screw every man in this stinking goddam town!"

I came awfully close to going over the dam right that second, but I pulled myself back from the brink. "Husbands and wives have agreed to disagree before, Mona," I said when I could speak. "They stay married, and they party around separately, but they do it discreetly."

"That's not my way," she announced flatly. "And my way is the way we do it, dear." The smile she gave me I carried in my memory for a long time. "Good night."

When she switched her bare ass out of the room and upstairs, I went back to the bottle. I marveled that she thought I was going to let her get away with it.

Three days later, I called Andy Martin to make arrangements to get the evidence I didn't need. Andy knew Tom Harrington, and he didn't want to take it on, but money talks, and when I reached three times his usual fee, he agreed to do it—provided his own testimony wasn't needed.

I'd already made up my mind that no one's testimony would be needed. If Mona was going to plead her case to her father, she'd have to do it from her grave.

The details took time to refine, but I had plenty of time.

Ten days after Lud and I came back from Nags Head, Wing drove in from the Edmonds Road job in the morning and we went office hunting together. Lud had been insistent that we had to get out of the office-in-a-hatband stage immediately. Actually, I had an office of sorts at home, but it wasn't the type of setup to impress anyone, and the house was up for sale, anyhow, since I was living at Lud's. When I'd asked Wing on the phone to come in that morning and told him why, he'd sounded glum but had raised no objection.

In a town like Moline there's never too much choice in the way of available office space, and by ten o'clock Wing and I were signing the lease. He had almost nothing to say during the proceedings. I noticed that his eyes were bloodshot and that his handsome features looked drawn. "Are you hitting the bottle?" I asked him as we left the realtor's office.

"I reckon I'm of age," he retorted. "But if you got to know, the answer is no, I'm not." He passed a hand over a blond shadow of beard stubble. "We got us a joker sprayin' our newly laid bituminous nights with kerosene, an' I been layin' out in the brush tryin' to ketch him at it."

Kerosene or gasoline on freshly laid bituminous asphalt cuts it to a point where the binding disintegrates completely. All kerosened sections would have to be done over. "Why the hell haven't you said something about it before?"

"Oh, I thought you'd be all taken up with your bride," he drawled. He waited to see if I would react; when I didn't, he went on again. "It's a penny-ante performance, more of a nuisance 'n anything else. So far, anyway. Type of thing that looks like somebody I fired is tryin' to get in a lick in return. I had a look through the payroll records at the names of those I had to let go recently, but none of 'em look like they got the moxie for this kind of thing."

"You don't think it's more serious than that?"

"More nuisance than anything," he repeated. "Havin' to go back an' patch and send the rollers over it again. The way he operates, the feller seems to know a little bit about bituminous. Mostly he picks sections the rubber-tired rollers have been over but before the steel rollers get the better compaction that would give us a more solid bind."

"Where's the watchman while all this is going on?"

"That's a powerful piece of country to cover in the dark. Even with me out there with him, an' us split up, the Kerosene Kid has slipped in on us twice. I figger he's got a tank slung on the back of his car an' darts in an' out on the fresh-laid sections from the mess of side roads out there. I been tempted to shut down one spreader an' limit his action, but I hate to do it."

"How bad has it been?"

"Oh, not bad. Prob'ly cost us half a day in man-hours fixin' up after the bastard. No real problem yet. Not that I wouldn't like to catch him at it."

"I'll meet you out there tonight and we'll try it again." Wing nodded. "No sense in your spreading yourself too thin trying to corral him by yourself. And speaking of being spread too thin—" I seized the opportunity to move into an area where I expected to have difficulty with Wing—"I'm wondering if that might not be true in other areas. We're carrying quite a load between us, and I've got bids in now on two more jobs I'm reasonably certain we're going to get." Wing smiled. "If we get even one of them, you and I won't be able to handle all the details alone. What would you think about bringing in a couple of people at the supervisory level? I talked to a boy the other day who's working for Lumenti, and I think he'd make us a good man. I'd like to have you talk to him, too, and see if you agree."

"Go ahead an' hire him," Wing said. He sounded dispirited. "I don't need to talk to him. What would I talk to him about? What do I know about an engineer's qualifications these days? I don't even talk the language of these kids comin' out've school." He had been staring moodily into space; he turned to look directly at me. "I've seen it comin'. Expand an' expand an' keep on expandin'. Bring in the young hotshots an' keep ol' Wing out in the weeds where he don't smell up the fancy office we just rented. D'you realize, Jim, that it's not so long ago our weekly payroll didn't match what we're payin' a month for that office?"

He said it with no anger but with a kind of despondent acceptance, and I didn't know what to say to him in reply. "Are you saying you'd prefer us to scratch along as a jerkwater outfit without two 'dozers to rub together and not knowing where its next job is coming from?" I asked finally.

"I don't know what I'm sayin'," he replied. "Or what I'd prefer." He sounded honestly troubled. "I liked it the way we had it, 'fore all this—all this big push. 'Course, I want the company to grow, too." He grinned halfheartedly. "Progress is a bitch, ain't she?"

"It's only the changeover period that's difficult." I tried to soothe him. "In three months you'll think we've always been doing it the new way."

"Yeah, mebbe so. I hope you're right. Well, anyway, no need for you to lose any sleep over this kerosene deal. I'll catch the booger."

"Never mind about my losing sleep. I may be late but I'll meet you there tonight. And if you get there first, look before you jump because I won't be wearing a sign."

He smiled, his first real smile since he'd driven into town. "You do the same, hoss. I'll be seein' you."

He climbed into his rattling Galaxie to drive back out to the job. I watched him go, and I was concerned. It wasn't the same, and we both knew it. The hell of it was I didn't know what it was going to take to make it the same. There didn't seem to be any easily-arrived-at solution.

I spent the next three nights staked out in the roadside brush on Edmonds Road. Wing and I were at opposite ends of a freshly paved section, and we changed our positions each night to correspond with the progress of the job. In the moonless dark, the silent earthmoving machinery bulked around us like prehistoric monsters. Not even an owl hooted the whole three nights. The fourth night I couldn't be there, and Wing called me the next morning to report that the marauder had sprayed kerosene in an irregular pattern over a quarter mile of asphalt.

"I'll get him," Wing promised grimly when I drove out to look at it. As he had said, it wasn't a major problem, but it was certainly a major annoyance. "An' when I do, he'll remember it awhile."

"I wish I could spend more time out here with you, Wing—"

"You got enough to do," he said shortly. "I'll get him."

I drove back to town trying to concentrate on more important problems, but the image of a kerosene-spraying unknown kept breaking up my chain of thought.

I promised myself I'd get back out there to give Wing a hand.

Lud's dinner party eventually expanded to include twenty-eight people, fourteen husbands and their wives, and it got off to a funereal start. We met the group in the formal drawing room, a large room unused except for special occasions. The conversation was stilted and there wasn't much of it. I was uncomfortable in a new suit that Lud had bulldozed the tailor into completing in time for the affair. Most of the men and their women ran to a pattern: large, sleek, whitehaired, and jowly. Lud and I were the youngest persons in the room.

Tom Harrington was there, standing a little apart. Lud had extended the invitation to him in person. She had reported that he hadn't seemed much impressed. I was pleased to see that none of the guests seemed impressed by him, an indication of how quickly it became noised about in circles like this that there was a new snout in the trough.

Lud was looking her best for the occasion, and her best was considerable. She had on a shimmering gown of some kind of gold froth, and her hairdresser had perspired over her for two hours that afternoon in the master bedroom. She had brought in two men to serve drinks and, whether it was the drinks or her own artful circulating, she had considerably raised the group temperature from its low, low point before we were summoned in to the catered dinner.

She had made her table arrangements carefully, too, after preparing a detailed scouting report on the invitees. She placed the dimmest social bulbs closest to herself at the table, thus assuring herself they'd receive the proper attention. At judicious intervals around the large oval table, she'd placed the more roguish gentlemen next to the liveliest ladies the group afforded. The talk and laughter emanating from these areas of vivacity eventually thawed the protective permafrost of the others, and by the time the second wine was served, everyone was contributing to the conversation. I watched Lud's sharp-eyed glances darting around the table as she stirred up the occasional dead spot with a smile and a query. She was working like a stevedore while still contriving to look like a Botticelli angel.

I had been placed between two of the older women, and I had been given my orders, which were to keep talking. "College is always a good subject," Lud had said. "Most of them have children and grandchildren in college, although the majority of them never went themselves."

"Too busy making money from the age of ten. What am I supposed to talk about? Nothing ever happened to me in college that you could print in a family newspaper."

"Make it up. Tell them about the time you disassembled a Model-T and lugged it up into the belfry of the chapel and reassembled it there. Tell them anything. They won't know the difference. I don't know why it is that politicians seem to flourish in inverse ratio to the amount of time they spent in school."

"Not politicians," I pointed out. "The men behind the politicians."

"Have it your way. But you keep talking. If I see your jaws stop wagging, I'll throw a biscuit at you."

I kept talking, but it was uphill work, one of the hardest day's work of my life. Both corseted old biddies had surveyed me glacially when I gallantly seated them at the opening of the meal. Neither touched her wine. Their whole attitude proclaimed forcefully that *they* were associating with a wife-murderer and political upstart under protest and only at the urgent behest of their spouses. I didn't break them down exactly, but at the cost of a wilted collar and a moist backbone I had them listening and contributing an occasional remark by the time we reached the dessert course. Just before it was served, Lud awarded me the Croix de Guerre with palms via a quick nod. I had already made up my mind that I was going to have a serious talk with her about this sort of affair, though. It just wasn't my line of work.

Lud signaled for the group's dispersal by rising. She shepherded the women back into the drawing room while I led the men into the library. One of the hired bartenders was dispensing brandy and cigars. "Damn fine dinner, Wilson," a redfaced giant I remembered from the drawing room as Ken Stackpole said to me as soon as the library doors closed. "Your wife's a real organizer. An' that pineapple upside-down cake was great. I'm s'posed to be on a diet"—he patted his gross stomach—"but you reckon yore man here could rustle me up an extra portion now my wife's out of sight?" He laughed heartily.

I turned to look for Lud's butler-bartender, but he had overheard and already anticipated me. He went to a side door and spoke briefly to someone outside it. In minutes, a tray was handed in to him with a dozen of the gooey desserts on it. They disappeared amidst the men, who were circling him like snow in the desert.

"Talk to you a minute, Wilson," Richie Hoey said at my elbow. " 'Fore this gang gets the sugar off its teeth."

He was a roly-poly little baldy who had a trick of bouncing up and down on his toes as he spoke. "You really got somethin' goin' for you here," he went on, glancing around the large room and running a gift cigar appreciatively under his nose. "How 'bout you drivin' over to my place some night soon an' meetin' with a few of us? Wouldn't tie you up long. Strictly business." He chuckled.

My interest rose. The few would be an important few. "Any time you say," I replied.

"Week from tonight? Only be three, four of us," he said deprecatingly.

"I'll be there."

"We'll count on it." Shrewd eyes studied me as I held a match for his cigar. "You seem better organized 'n most men your age, Wilson." He turned away without waiting for a reply.

Two different men had mentioned organization just minutes apart. I'd always prided myself on my own ability to coordinate things properly, and Lud seemed just as capable in her own domain. It put a different picture on the situation. I was going to have to revise my objections to the stuffiness of the atmosphere at dinner if that was what it took to reach the business-as-usual stage with Richie Hoey and his friends during the brandy-and-cigars aftermath. I was just going to have to learn to put up with it.

I moved through the room putting into practice another bit of Lud's coaching. Three days before, she'd given me a set of pictures of the men who were to be present, together with a brief item on each, regarding spheres of influence and special interests. As per her instructions, I circulated among the clustered groups of men, fitting faces to names, dropping a word here and there about a special interest. When little pockets of discussion flared up, drawing others into the conversation, I moved on to another group. Twice in my progress around the room I saw Tom Harrington standing in a corner, alone. I didn't go near him. I was surprised that he'd come at all. With what I represented to him, I didn't see how he could afford to be there. I made a note to ask Lud how she had persuaded him.

The room became a beehive of animated, arm-waving groups, and the butler-bartender finally had to tell us that the ladies were waiting for us. En route to rejoin them, Richie Hoey winked at me and grinned. I didn't catch his particular meaning if he had one, but it was indication enough that the entire dinner had gone well.

Lud thought so, too, in the post-affair rehash conducted upstairs in my bedroom. I was sitting in a low-slung chair, dressed in T-shirt and trousers, and Lud was perched on the edge of my bed with her legs tucked up beneath her after having kicked her shoes off. "The women liked you," she was saying. "You don't have charm, but you have force, and sometimes it's almost as good. They all came prepared to dislike you, but you brought them at least part way around. How did you make out with the men?"

I told her about Richie Hoey's invitation, and she listened intently. "That's what we need," she declared when I finished, nodding her blonde head vigorously. "We're on our way, no doubt about it. Next Saturday? I must remember to cancel our table at the country club dance. Too bad in a way; I was going to use it as an opportunity to test the climate of public opinion locally. But first things first. By the way, how did Tom make out?"

"He'll be a week thawing out."

"He's been an intimate friend of those men for years," she protested.

"Maybe it's a case of 'What have you done for me lately?' " I said. "Anyway, they froze him. I don't see why he came at all. What kind of arm-twisting did you have to use to get him to agree? With me at the head of the table, his position was impossible."

Her brows were knitted in a frown. "It wasn't too difficult," she said absently. The frown disappeared, and she leaned back on her elbows, relaxed, looking as soft and appealing as I'd ever seen her look. Before I could press for an explanation, she rose from the bed suddenly and padded over to me in her stockinged feet. "Jim—"

"No," I cut her off instantly.

"No? No what?"

"No snuggling."

The corners of her mouth drew down, then lifted in a conscious effort at a smile. "You'd make a poor shopper at a bargain sale, Jim. How do you know the merchandise is no good until you've tried it?"

"The merchandise doesn't do anything for me."

"No?" She arched herself up on her toes and began a slow pirouette, her breasts jutting boldly. "Perhaps if I—"

"No. Rack it up and drag it out of here, Lud."

She came down off her toes. For a long, silent moment she stared at me, then whirled and stalked from the room, slamming the door so viciously the bureau mirror vibrated, and five seconds later a picture slowly slid down the opposite wall.

I left my chair, picked up her forgotten shoes, and put them outside in the hall.

CHAPTER X

THREE NIGHTS later, I stopped in at Veronica's apartment. She seemed surprised to see me. "Let's go out to the cabin," she suggested when it got through to her what I wanted.

"I don't have time," I said.

We went to bed, and while it was good for me, I'd have had to be a wooden Indian not to know that it hadn't been for her. She threw on a robe and followed me out to the door when I was dressed. "Do me a favor, Jim," she said. "Don't come back again."

I had the door open already; I closed it. "What the hell do you mean 'Don't come back again'?"

"What I said." She was pale but her voice was under control. "I'm not a whore, and I won't be used like one."

"Just because I'm busy now—"

"You're going to be busy from now on. And you're

129

m-married, and everything—everything's different." She was crying, her face all twisted.

I stood there thinking of fifteen different things to say, and wound up saying none of them. I opened the door again and left the apartment. I stormed down the corridor and, ignoring the elevator, ran down the stairs to the sidewalk. I'd just turned toward the station wagon, which was parked half a dozen cars from the building entrance, when I saw a man step backward quickly into the shadows of a doorway across the street. It was so dark I couldn't get much of an indication of size or shape, let alone individuality, but I had an impression that he limped. As I took my first steps away from the entrance, I turned my head and watched from the corner of my eye. The man emerged from the doorway and began paralleling my progress, across the street and a few yards behind me, and he was definitely limping. I walked past the station wagon without even looking toward it. In my present mood, I welcomed the opportunity to come to grips with something I could hook my hands into.

Half a block farther on, the shadower crossed the street and took up the pursuit directly behind me but still some distance away. I turned right at the first corner and stepped into the interior of the first doorway. If it was Garvey following me, as I halfway thought it might be, I knew he was too cute to be caught hugging the building wall in his tailing. I was prepared to go out into the middle of the street after him if necessary, but the shadow hurrying past my doorway was so close that I could have touched him. I still couldn't see his face. I caught him in ten yards and neck-chopped him. He heard me coming but couldn't turn around in time. He went so spraddle-legged that I was sure it wasn't Garvey. I grabbed him as he started to fall and muscled him back up the street into the doorway. The diffused light from a window display illuminated the pale, startled features of Whit Bailey, Mona's inamorata the day I'd killed her. I hadn't set eyes on him since. I didn't know who was the more surprised, Bailey or me. "What are you doing following me?" I yelled at him, holding him up by his lapels.

"Noth—nothing." He got it out around a bobbing Adam's apple. He lifted a hand to rub the back of his neck gingerly. "You—you're imagining things."

"The hell I'm imagining things. What's the idea, Bailey?"

His weak, good-looking features seemed shriveled. "You're—you're mistaken, that's all. You're—"

I backhanded him across the face, left-right, left-right. "Tell me again I'm mistaken," I challenged. He shrank back against the store window looking so much like a frightened rabbit that I felt disgusted. "This was never your idea, Bailey. What are you doing here and who put you up to it?"

He moistened his lips with a quick flirt of his tongue. "I—no one put me up to it. I tell you you're mistaken—" I raised my hand again, and he flinched. "Ludmilla!" he blurted out.

"*Ludmilla?*" I echoed incredulously. "You mean she— oh, yes, I begin to see." In view of her ultimatum to me about tomcatting, Ludmilla obviously had decided to keep herself informed. But Whit Bailey, for God's sake? "You silly bastard, how did you think you were going to get away with it? You couldn't shadow a blind—" I stopped abruptly as something occurred to me. I took another look at Whit Bailey. "Say, are you the one spraying kerosene on unset asphalt out at Edmonds Road?"

"Of—of course not," he said too quickly.

"You're not a silly bastard, you're a damn fool idiot, Bailey," I said with conviction. "If Wing Darlington ever catches you at it, he'll pour so much of your own kerosene up your ass you'll need a plastic rectum." I shook him until his head bobbed and his shoulders bounced off the door frame. "Now what's all this about Lud?"

"She—she came to me and said she—she wanted to know what you were up to nights," he mumbled.

"And you didn't have any better sense than to try to find out. What made you listen to her?"

"Ludmilla has always been a good friend of mine." He

131

tried to make it sound dignified, but it came out as a pathetic little whimper.

The more I thought of it, the less possible it sounded. After his run-in with me at the motel, Bailey shouldn't have wanted any part of me. There was something very much out of line in his protestations. "How does Lud happen to be such a friend of yours?"

Despite my grip on him, he had one hand free enough to wave it helplessly. "She's—just a good friend."

"The hell she is. Friendship would never send you on this errand, man. I could have killed you that day and been justified, and you know it, but here you are, sucking around. Why?"

"She said—she insisted you wouldn't dare do anything to me now, even if you—even if you caught me at it."

"She did, did she?" Lud thought that I'd feel I had too much to lose. "Let me tell you something, Bailey—" I stopped and reconsidered. This type at the end of my arm wasn't much excuse for a man, but he was demonstrably available and there ought to be some way I could make use of him. I groped for an instant, and then the germ of an idea came to me. "Since you're already a secret agent, why don't we take the logical step and make a double agent out of you? I've got a little job you can do for me."

"Oh, I couldn't! I mean—well, Ludmilla wouldn't like it at all!"

I shook him, and he gasped.

"What was that again?"

"Please! I'd be—I'd be no good at it, anyway."

He was certainly right about that. And with him in Ludmilla's pocket anyhow, too great a risk would be involved. It was still nagging at me that I'd never had the time to do anything about finding out who had tampered with George Pierson's car. For a second I'd considered impressing Bailey into service in that connection, but if he even mentioned it to Lud, the lid would be off for fair. And using Bailey would be the equivalent of a halfway measure or less. It was time I got on the stick and did something about it myself, instead of making excuses that I didn't have the time.

I could feel Bailey trembling in my hands. It was a funny thing, but even with the kerosene and all, I couldn't really seem to get mad at the guy. He might have been hell on wheels in bed with a woman, but in every other way that mattered, he was such a no-count type as a man that he was almost pitiful. About to turn him loose, I thought of something else. Lud must have a powerful grip on this one where it hurt to have him risk following me. "What does Lud have on you, Bailey?"

"N-nothing." He wet his lips again. "She's—she's just a good friend." I moved my right hand slightly, and he jerked backward involuntarily. The words popped out of him like seeds from a crushed watermelon. "There was a slight—ah—problem with one of the secretaries at the bank. She—she had a baby. Ludmilla handled everything and—and kept it quiet."

The classic squeeze, I thought. I let go of Bailey, and his hands went automatically to his clothes, smoothing out the bunched-up fabric where I'd been holding him. He looked at me hopefully. "You can run along," I decided. "But if I hear of another drop of kerosene being spread around out on Edmonds Road, I'm coming looking for you. Understand?" He nodded fearfully. "All right. Blow."

He limped three steps in the direction from which he'd come.

"Bailey!" I called. He stopped instantly. "What about this limp? Is it from the bullets I put in your butt?"

He spoke without turning around. "The doctor says it's a muscle pull that will ease in time as it heals thoroughly."

"Glad to hear it. I wouldn't want to have marred your beauty." He probably thought I was being facetious, and on one level I certainly was, but I really meant it. The Baileys of the world had enough of a load to carry without an additional contribution from me. I'd used him as an instrument to bring down Mona, but I actually

133

had nothing against him personally. If it hadn't been him, it would have been someone else.

He started to walk away from me again, slowly, as if afraid I'd call him back. I didn't say anything, and he speeded up. I watched him hurry around the corner and disappear from view. It might have turned out to be a profitable evening, I decided. At the very least, Bailey was a stick to beat Ludmilla with. And, even indebted to her as he was, I had no real fear of his following me again.

I walked back to the station wagon, intending to drive straight home and have it out with her. I might not be able to get mad at Bailey, but I had no difficulty at all in getting mad at her. If she thought she was going to regulate my private life, she had another think coming, and the sooner she found it out, the better.

Three blocks from the house, I passed Mueller's Service Station, where all the Pierson cars were serviced, and it reminded me again of George Pierson's Thunderbird. On impulse, I wheeled in to the gas pumps. It was late enough so that only a single attendant was on duty. I knew that the place was busy enough in the daytime to keep three men employed. It wasn't impossible that one of them knew something about the Thunderbird that he wasn't talking about. In Moline, people grew up learning not to talk about things unless there was a reason for talk.

"Evenin', Mr. Wilson." The young fellow who came out of the office greeted me cheerfully. "Fill it up?"

"Yes," I said. I didn't know the young fellow, but he knew me. It made my question easier when he finished filling the tank and handed me a credit card ticket to sign. "I imagine you had a run of people checking their cars to make sure they weren't going to run off the road," I said casually. "After the accident a while back." He nodded. "I've been meaning to have the wagon checked, as a matter of fact. D'you have a minute to do it now?"

"Sure thing, Mr. Wilson. Pull in on the hoist and I'll have a look."

I backed up, swung around, and drove up on the

134

metal tracks. When I got out of the car, the attendant gave it the air and the wagon rose to shoulder height. He stepped under it and at once began checking the steering mechanism. I purposely hadn't mentioned steering mechanism to him, but he'd gone directly to it. Evidently it was no secret what had sent the Pierson car off the road that night. No secret around the Mueller Service Station, anyway. What I needed, I thought, was an attendant who showed reluctance to admit that he had such knowledge, which could be an indication that he had knowledge he was afraid to talk about. I'd have to keep trying with the other attendants at the station and see what I drew.

"Looks fine, Mr. Wilson," the boy said at last, emerging from under the wagon.

"Fine," I echoed. He lowered the hoist and I got back into the wagon and drove home. Or more correctly, drove to Ludmilla's. It never felt like a home to me, and I doubted that it ever would. I parked in the double garage and went into the house. When I entered her bedroom, Lud was sound asleep. I turned on her bedside table lamp, and at the onslaught of light, she stirred and flung an arm across her eyes, then removed it and looked up at me. She looked cool and fresh. "What is it?" she asked, sitting up quickly. "What's happened?" Her nightgown appeared to be the same lacy confection she'd worn on our wedding night or its twin.

"I caught Whit Bailey following me tonight," I said. "If I catch him again, I'll tie you down over the end of this bed and take a yard of skin off you with my belt."

She swung herself up from the bed and onto her feet after throwing back the sheet. "Any time you think you can intimidate—"

"I don't know why you took the trouble," I interposed. "I'd have told you if you asked me."

"I assume he found you in the bed of Cartwright's fat secretary," she said calmly.

I wasn't going to give her the satisfaction of knowing that that was over. "He found me where I wanted to be,

135

Lud. And where I intend to be whenever I feel like it."

She shook her head. "No, Jim. No. Your freewheeling days are over. You've got an image to build. There'll be no more of that sort of thing."

The sight of her standing there imperiously cool, handing out dictums, infuriated me. "Damn you, I'll do as I please! I told you beforehand—"

"We both want the same thing, and conduct of that nature jeopardizes it," she said coldly. "I can't permit it. If I—"

"You can't permit it," I snorted. "I suppose the next step is for you to tell Veronica to get out of town?"

"If necessary."

The full-armed facial slap I dealt her sent her reeling backward until she sprawled ungracefully on the bed. She rebounded from it while the sharp sound was still in the air, and came after me like a lynx after a snowshoe rabbit, her long fingernails hooked like claws. I left-hooked her to the ribcage, grabbed her by an arm and a leg as she sagged, picked her up, and threw her at the bed. She landed on her back, gasping, the lace covering a third of her. I took hold of its trailing edges and drew it all the way up her body, bagging her head in its loose folds. I ignored her kicking as I flattened her out, nude from her throat to her painted toenails. Starting with rape, I intended to use and abuse her deliberately in every way known to man. This one needed to be shown who was in charge.

Holding her down with one hand, I ripped off my clothes with the other. I climbed onto the bed with her and had no sooner forcefully split her flesh than I received the first of a series of shocks. She wasn't fighting me. The muffled sounds emanating from beneath the enveloping nightgown were not protests. Instead of the limp, inanimate flesh to which Mona had accustomed me, I was riding a furious, totally knowledgeable pinwheel whose surging, fiery reaction instantly deflected my purpose. How do you beat down a woman who welcomes your assault? Several times, the frenetically savage conflict teetered us on the edge of the bed. When I finally exploded in a draining burst that restored me to some semblance of sanity, I withdrew slowly and rose to my feet. Lud was sprawled loosely, her friction-marked thighs still twitching, and her breasts rising and falling rapidly. In a moment both her hands went up and swept the confining folds of her nightgown from her head. "I *told* you—Mona was—the lesbian," she panted.

I left her bedroom without saying a word.

The experience had shaken all my deep-seated convictions. Ludmilla Pierson-Wilson represented a clear and present danger of a type other than I'd imagined. A man could get altogether too fond of what I'd just had, and I couldn't afford to give the woman another hold on me.

In my own room, I made up my mind. I'd never get back into bed with her again.

Late Saturday afternoon I drove the two hundred miles to Richie Hoey's home and arrived in the early evening. His house, a large but unpretentious white frame dwelling with green gables, was almost in the center of town. It had a postage-stamp-sized lawn in front. Sam Carstens answered the chime at the door, and we exchanged greetings. "Meetin's in the front room," he announced.

I followed him into an old-fashioned "front room" that reminded me of my uncle's house. The wallpaper looked as if it had been in place for fifty years. Ugly, rust-colored draperies closed out most of the light from the small-paned windows, and the fireplace andirons were black, wrought-iron barking dogs. Four heavy armchairs were drawn up in a hollow square, and in front of each was a collapsible television tray. To one side, a tea caddy had been pressed into service as a portable bar.

"Drink?" Sam asked me.

"I believe I'll wait for the others, Sam."

"Here's the boss now," Sam said.

Richie bustled in behind a ten-inch cigar, and Sam left the room. The little round man shook hands energetically,

137

motioned me to one of the chairs, and perched his own fat rump on the edge of another. "Well, now, how's things at your end of the state?" he began, in what was apparently a familiar opening gambit.

"If the goose hung any higher, my only worry would be about someone removing the rope."

He chuckled agreeably and took a drag on his cigar. "I asked you to come a half hour earlier 'n the others, Wilson, because I thought it was time for a little talk between you an' me. Plain talk." He waved the cigar at me. "There's items you haven't taken sufficiently into consideration, so to speak, some of 'em in your own backyard. Most of 'em going back to the fact that of the group at your wife's dinner party the other night, while none of us were politicians in the strict sense of the word, we tell the politicians what to do." He chuckled again, but at once turned serious.

"Now you're a maverick to a lot of the people I talk to, Wilson. You didn't come up through the ranks, an' you're askin' to step in at the top level. I know you done some right smart pushin' an' bangin' in your area to shape things up the way you think they ought to be, but ordinarily you wouldn't have the chance of a crystal ball in a hailstorm. It's a combination of circumstances, plus you bein' the right man—the available man—at the right time, at least to my way of thinkin', that's got you this far. But to get down to cases, there's a missin' link in your operation."

He paused as if awaiting a comment, so I supplied it. "I wasn't aware of it."

"I figgered you wasn't," he said, nodding his bald head emphatically. "Now I been helpin' things to happen the way I want 'em to happen in this county for a good long time, an' I know that power flows to the man gutsy enough to step in an' grab its tail. You've done that, but out've channels. We may not be politicians, but we work with politicians. An' there's no lone wolves; we work together."

He took another drag on the cigar, whose ash whitened an additional quarter inch. "At the county level, Wilson," he resumed, "when all's said an' done, *everything* traces to politics, all up an' down the line. Tom Harrington was wired in politically all over the state, which was the reason the boys went along with him even after they begun to look a little cross-eyed at some of his goin's-on. Up to now, at least, you don't seem to have paid any attention to the grass roots of the political situation in your county, an' I didn't get the impression the other night that even that whip-smart wife of yours had given it a thought." He paused. "Scares me a little, that wife of yours," he confided. "Glad it ain't me has to ride herd on her. Although from the shape of your saddle horn, you're the man for the job. I think." His pause this time was for effect. "Men in these parts don't take kindly to pushy women. But then I'm not givin' you any news."

"There'll be no problem," I replied to the implied warning. I steered him back to what I considered to be the main point. "Now this political situation—"

"Yeah." He leaned back in his chair and crossed his short legs. "In Albermarle County, Harrington had split off from the organization, so to speak, an' there was some feelin' about it. We'd like to see you work with the organization."

"I've always voted—"

"Sure you've always voted the ticket. I'm not talkin' about that, or about contributions. I'm talkin' about sittin' down with the people in Albermarle County who count an' workin' closely enough with them an' with us so there's no chance of cross-purposes bobbin' up at embarrassin' times." He peered at me through a thin haze of blue cigar smoke. "When you get back to Moline, I'd call it a personal favor if you'd sit down like you are here with me an' talk to a man I believe you'd find right congenial in a lot of respects."

"In Moline? Who's the man?"

"Sig Jacobus."

"I know Sig," I said slowly. A number of things came into focus more sharply at the sound of the name: the coolness between Harrington and Jacobus, an item or two of gossip around town that I'd never tied together, and the lack of cooperation between Sig and Harrington's pet prosecutor at the coroner's hearing after Mona's death. I'd always known that Sig dabbled in politics, of course, but never to what extent. The big question in my mind bore on one fact: if I sat down with him, who would be telling whom? "Not well, but I know him," I went on. "He and Harrington had a difference of opinion a couple of years ago."

"They did that," Richie agreed. "An' affairs in Albermarle County been goin' to hell in a handbasket ever since. We been hurtin' there. Even in his best days, Harrington was always bullheaded, an' when a man been on top as long as he has, he's made enough enemies so some chickens got to come home to roost." He pointed the half-smoked cigar at me. "You got a lot of gumph, Wilson, an' you ain't put a foot down wrong yet, but you couldn't have done what you have in Albermarle County if Harrington 'd been able to call on the backin' he'd have had as recently as a year ago. His attitude lately done cancelled all promissory notes."

"I'll be glad to talk to Sig," I said. I wasn't sure that I would be, but it was obviously the thing to say. "I've never been a politically-minded type, and I don't know what I could contribute, specifically. I'm not—"

"You don't need to worry about contributin'," Richie interrupted. "Sig 'll just want to know you're on the team. He calls a meetin' every little while, an' you'll sit in an' catch up on the facts of life in your area." He grinned at me. "Just like we'll do for the state here this evenin'. With you, the cart comes before the horse, boy, because you happened to come along at a time when a few people could take an interest in you. Another time it could've been a whole hell of a lot different, I can tell you. Why, it took me—"

He stopped as the chimes sounded at the front door. In a moment Sam Carstens ushered in the dessert-loving big man of Lud's dinner party. I groped for his name and then it came to me: Ken Stackpole. We shook hands. "Glad to see you again, Wilson," Stackpole boomed.

140

"Didn't happen to bring along any of that pineapple upside-down cake with you, did you?"

"Sam 'll bring you in a wedge of apple pie my youngest daugher, Nina, made," Richie promised him. "It'll run your blood pressure up to where Doc Sanders 'll rule you off the track."

"He's had me on a diet for fifteen years," Stackpole laughed. He glanced around. "Where's—ah, here he is," he said as the chimes sounded again. Another man I'd seen at Lud's party but to whom I hadn't paid much attention entered behind Sam. The newcomer was a stringy, attenuated individual with wispy gray hair and obvious false teeth. "Bob Jessup, Jim Wilson," said Richie, reintroducing us. "Let's sit down an' get to work, boys. Sam, you can bring in the trays now."

We were barely in our chairs when Sam wheeled in a cart with four large trays on it. In quick succession, he placed each on one of the folding tables beside our chairs. Each tray contained two massive roast beef sandwiches, a huge section of apple pie with a slice of cheese aboard it, and a pot of coffee. Richie did all the talking as we ate, but somehow he managed to clean up his own tray as quickly as the rest of us who had been eating in silence.

Carstens returned and removed everything except the coffee pots, then set up a gateleg table in the center of the hollow square around which we were sitting. When he left the room that time, I heard the click of a lock in the door. Richie went to a desk and unlocked its center drawer, removed a map, which he brought back to the table, and spread it out carefully, smoothing out its creases. I leaned forward to see better, and despite my background, it took me a couple of minutes to recognize what I was looking at.

On a detailed map that featured the road networks of the state, lines had been drawn in various colors. Red, blue, and green lines predominated in the color scheme, with the red lines representing past highway construction projects and the blue lines representing current ones. That left the green lines to represent future projects, and my eyes automatically sought out the location of Albemarle County. I could see highway routes marked in, that I knew as a practical measure couldn't exist for five years. This planning board certainly took the long-range view.

"This is for your benefit, Jim," Richie said to me, picking up a black marking crayon. With practiced ease, he sketched bold lines onto the map, dividing the state into four roughly equal sectors. "This is the way we been operatin'," he continued, whirling the map until it faced me squarely. "As a practical thing, we don't have but so much influence at the capitol, but since there's always good ol' boys up there whose interests coincide with some of ours, there's a general unanimity in the backscratchin' that goes on. Even on state jobs we can usually count on bein' consulted. Unofficially, of course. The county jobs don't always come out even, of course, so once in a while we cross borders accordin' to who's had the latest slice of pie." He winked heavily. "We ration out the jobs amongst the boys you saw at the dinner party plus a few others, an' we try to have a couple of jobs a year go to an 'outside' construction firm in our own counties to keep some sharp newspaper editor from hollerin' 'monopoly.' "

I could see from the black-lined map that Richie's slice of pie was the largest, while Albermarle County and its surrounding area was the smallest, and I suspected there had been some readjustments since the last map-drawing, but I didn't say anything. A man has to walk before he can run. I didn't say much of anything for the balance of the meeting, which lasted an hour and a half. I listened while Richie skillfully dictated the assignment of county construction projects budgeted for the next twelve-month period. There was no disagreement; an occasional question was always speedily and satisfactorily disposed of. The aggregate figures were enough to make my head swim. Accustomed as I was to dealing with a job at a time, and never the largest job, it seemed to me at times that Richie was dealing with the national budget.

"None of us are foolish enough or hungry enough to

142

want *all* the jobs in our territories," Richie explained to me at one point. "But we keep our crews busy, an' when somethin' with a little extra cream in it comes along, we usually ain't behind the door when it gets handed out."

By the time the meeting broke up, I had an increased ration of respect for the other members of the little group. Despite his verbosity and general air of country bumpkinship, Richie was a remarkably sharp man with a pencil. Ken Stackpole, drinking coffee steadily and burping just as steadily, raised only an occasional point, but each one cut to the bone. Jessup contributed almost nothing verbally, but sat back almost as if he was a spectator, rather than a participant.

Richie detained me at the front door as the others departed. "Well?" he demanded. "Learn anything?"

"I'm going to have to go back to school," I said. "A lot of it came too fast."

He nodded. "You'll catch up. You've got a good solid foundation. I checked out a couple of your jobs, from bids to completion, before I drove over to your wife's dinner party." He grinned. "Nothin' that could pull the roof down on us quicker than a man in the combine doin' shoddy work that could get us investigated by the legislature." He jerked a thumb at Jessup's lean figure getting into a car that was anything but a late model. "What'd you think of him?"

"He didn't seem to have much to say."

"He don't need to," Richie smiled. "Man could buy an' sell all of us with his loose change. Well—I'm plannin' on bein' over your way again in a week or ten days, Wilson. What would you think of us droppin' in on Sig together over a cup of coffee?"

"Fine," I said. "An hour's notice is all I'll need."

He walked with me out to my car. "Don't worry about nothin' meantime," he said.

"I'm not a worrier, Richie."

He cackled. "I did have that notion," he admitted.

We shook hands, and I drove back to Moline and Lud's house. It was two in the morning when I arrived, but she was waiting up for me. When I came in, she was in the

143

downstairs sitting room in a lime green negligee. "How did it go?" she asked before I was well inside the door.

"It was an eye-opener," I said. "I thought I was doing it all by myself around here, but I found out tonight I was doing a great deal of it on sufferance. The boys had become disenchanted with Harrington. Six months earlier or six months later and they might have squashed me like a mosquito. These people think BIG. We've got to adjust our sights upward."

"I *knew* it would be like that," she said with satisfaction. "Tom Harrington was always so close-mouthed about it, but I was positive there must be a small executive group that made the decisions. Tell me all about it."

"I want to take a shower," I protested.

"Then come ahead and take it. You can talk at the same time." She led the way upstairs and carried a straight-backed chair into the bathroom in my bedroom. "Go ahead," she repeated, seating herself.

I began the story while stripping off my clothes. In the shower I raised my voice above the hiss of the water as I continued to give her the details. "So Richie will be over soon and we'll sit down with Sig," I concluded, shutting off the water and reaching for a towel.

There was a silence. "I don't think I like that," Lud said at last. I leaned out of the shower stall to take a look at her, and she was frowning. "Why do we need Sig Jacobus?"

"Because that's the way the system works," I said. "If Harrington couldn't buck it, do you think we can?"

"Yes, I do," she said confidently. "Perhaps not tomorrow, but in time. We won't work outside the organization; we'll *be* the organization. I never thought Sig Jacobus was overly endowed with brains, anyhow."

Here was a prime example of what Richie had indirectly been warning me against. "Don't get the bit in your teeth, Lud. These men don't care for assertive females."

"Do you think I don't know it? Those old fuddyduddies exasperate me. Why do you think I needed you at all?"

144

She hurried on past that point. "But if we manage it properly, we'll be dictating to Richie Hoey in a couple of years, and not the other way around."

I made no reply to that piece of bombast. For a species supposed to be practical, women show damn little evidence of it at times. Lud was clever enough—every question she'd asked about the meeting had been of a penetrating nature—but she still really had no idea of what made the wheels go around in the state.

When I stepped out of the shower stall, the bathroom was empty. She must have left it only seconds before I did, but when I walked into the bedroom, she was stretched out on the bed and the lime-green negligee and anything that had been beneath it had disappeared. Despite a coating of powder, dull-looking blue bruises still mottled her thighs. I walked over and looked down at her as she stared up at me with an expression I couldn't define. "No," I said.

She came up off the bed like a panther, first to her knees in the middle of it, and then in a follow-through that was all one smooth-flowing motion off the bed onto her feet. "What do you mean, 'No'?"

"What I said. No more of that."

"Why not? What's the matter with you?"

"I'm afraid of you."

"A likely story!" She put her hand on my biceps. "Come on, Jim. This is the frosting on the cake. Let's not throw it away. We're partners, aren't we? Let's *be* partners." She made an impatient gesture when I didn't move. "Don't you trust me?"

"Since you mention it, no."

"That's ridiculous. You're in control and you know it. And I'm the best you ever had in bed and you know that, too." All the old arrogance was back in her voice.

"You're close, anyway, and that's part of the point. Suppose I got to like it too well? It might affect my judgement in regard to you. I'm not sure I could afford to have that happen."

"Of all the childish—!" She snatched my right hand

in hers and drew it down her naked body. "Can you tell me you don't want to?"

"No, but I can tell you I'm not going to."

She smothered all but the first syllable of the acid-tipped retort that sprang to her lips, then almost ran from the bedroom.

In the morning I found her nightgown and the lime-green negligee balled up in the corner where she'd pitched them.

It irked me that she had been so coolly confident that I'd return to her bed at the snap of her fingers. But even more, it disturbed me to find out during the dialogue how much I wanted to.

CHAPTER XI

AND SO, for ninety days, peace and progress reigned on all fronts.

There was no more trouble out on the job, and there was no more trouble with Ludmilla. She still showed flashes of her customary imperiousness, but as if realizing how much it irritated me, she quickly turned it off. Together we planned and saw through several social gatherings, which we arranged to best promote our interests with the right people. Richie Hoey came over to Moline, and he and I called on Sig Jacobus, who seemed satisfied. Even Richie seemed satisfied, although he once more found occasion to mention strong-minded wives.

I had run through the car-on-the-hoist gimmick with all the attendants at Mueller's. Only one of them had given me a blank stare and asked for specifics on what I wanted. He was a part-timer, a moonlighting school teacher named Graham Sawyer, and I didn't know if he honestly wasn't around the station enough to hear what was going on, or if he had a reason for playing dumb. Being a part-timer, he had irregular hours, and although I took to dropping by the station nights trying to catch him on alone, it hadn't worked out.

Harrington was still in the wings, but scarcely a menace, I felt. At another meeting of the brain trust, Richie and his friends had tossed us a substantial bone in the way of a job I hadn't expected to get, one on which we stood to make a real dollar. Wing was still acting standoffish with me, but the situation with him at least was no worse.

And that was how things stood on the evening Veronica telephoned me at Lud's house.

CHAPTER XII

IT WAS a Friday evening, and I'd returned to the house after a gruelling day spent out on the Edmonds Road site with Wing. On the way in, I'd stopped at Mueller's and left the station wagon to be serviced. I asked to have it brought to the house when it was ready, since I had to go out again. Sig Jacobus had asked me to stop in at his place for a few minutes. I walked the three blocks from Mueller's to Lud's place. I'd noticed her car at the service station, too, but she wasn't at home. The housekeeper, Margaret, didn't seem to be around, either. There was no message from Lud, but that wasn't unusual.

The Edmonds Road job was in its final stages, and I'd been working out with Wing the logistics for the transfer of our heavy equipment to the next job, which was to be half again as big. Whether it was from absorbing more sun than I'd been used to recently or from neglecting to eat, I arrived at the house with a headache. In the kitchen, I looked over the contents of the refrigerator, sliced off a couple of pieces of ham and made a sandwich, opened up a bottle of beer and a can of peaches, and made a standing-up meal. The whole house was quiet as I ate.

While waiting for the station wagon to be delivered, I went upstairs and began rechecking a set of figures at a makeshift desk I'd set up in a corner of my bedroom.

The headache grew worse, and I stretched out on the bed for a few minutes to see if that would help. It didn't, and I decided that if my head was going to ache it might as well have a reason. I went back downstairs to the kitchen and opened up another bottle of beer.

As I turned away from the refrigerator I saw through the kitchen window Lud's car backing into our driveway. A white-coveralled attendant in a long-billed work cap got out and walked toward the house, the car keys in his hand. It was customary for attendants delivering the cars to drop the keys just inside the back door. I opened the door just as he reached the top step. "Is the station wagon nearly ready?" I asked, realizing for the first time that the attendant was Graham Sawyer, the moonlighting school teacher.

He looked disconcerted at the sight of me standing there. "Mrs. Wilson came in, in a big hurry a few moments ago, sir," he said. "Her car wasn't ready right then, but the station wagon was, so she took it instead."

That was like Lud, too. If she had someplace to go and no transportation at hand, she was perfectly capable of walking out into the middle of the street and stopping the first car that came along and asking—demanding, rather—that it take her to her destination. I held out my hand for the keys. Sawyer gave them to me and turned to leave. "Come inside a minute," I said to him. "I want to talk to you."

The way my head felt, the statement was less true than it had been any time in the past four months, probably, but the combination of the empty house and his arrival alone seemed too good to pass up. It certainly gave me a chance at him that I hadn't been able to contrive at the station.

He hesitated before entering with obvious reluctance as I held the door for him. "I'll get grease on everything," he muttered as I closed the door. He was a mousy little man, and he had taken off his long-billed cap upon entering and stood turning it around and around in his hands.

"Don't worry about it, Sawyer. Have a beer?"

"No, thanks, Mr. Wilson."

"Sit down."

He sat stiffly, plainly wishing he were elsewhere. I sat down opposite him. I couldn't see any point in beating about the bush. If there was nothing to be learned from this man about George Pierson's car, then there was nothing to be learned from anyone at Mueller's. I was convinced of that. Acutally, the situation in general made the whole matter seem a lot less pressing than it had been originally, but with the opportunity squarely in hand—

"I asked you a question indirectly before," I began, "and you evaded a direct answer. I'll ask it plainly now, and I expect an answer. Did you ever see or hear of anyone tampering with George Pierson's car prior to his accident? Before you answer, I want you to know I've done some investigating since I talked to you last."

"No, sir, I never saw or heard of anything like that."

He said it so promptly and so positively that I was almost convinced. He sensed my mood; he had his cap halfway to his head and was rising from his chair when I spoke again. "The subject bothers you though, doesn't it, Sawyer? Why?"

"No reason, sir. I mean, it doesn't bother me."

But it did. My next question seemed to frame itself. "Did you ever see anything out of the ordinary take place in connection with that car?"

And he hesitated. He didn't know how much I knew. I waited while he made two false starts and began over again. "Not really," he said at last.

"Tell me about this business that was not really out of the ordinary, Sawyer."

He had settled back in his chair at my renewed questioning of him. He leaned forward in it, blinking at me. He wasn't wearing glasses, but he had a myopic look, as if he needed them. "I don't think you appreciate my position, Mr. Wilson," he said earnestly. There was a note of harried apprehension in his voice. "I have a wife and family, and I'm trying to get along. Anything I say to you—a wild guess, *anything*—if you act on it, depending upon the outcome, I'm going to have you or the other man mad at me and I can't afford that. It isn't as if I *saw* anything."

I had listened to this with growing impatience. I rose to my feet. "Cut the crap, Sawyer. Talk."

He gulped, then spoke hurriedly. "I saw the man who drove the Thunderbird away from the station that night. And that's all I saw."

"You mean it wasn't George Pierson?"

"That's right. The car had been in for servicing, and it was supposed to be delivered, but I was on duty alone. The telephone rang, and I had to take it inside. I heard a car start up, and by leaning around a corner of the desk, I could see the T-bird moving out." He paused. "Except for what happened afterward, I wouldn't have thought anything about it. Someone's always coming in for a car if we're late with it, like Mrs. Wilson did tonight."

"Who took the car, Sawyer?"

I expected him to say Lud, but for a second I thought he wasn't going to answer at all. "Mr. Darlington," he said finally.

"Mr.—Darlington? You mean Wing Darlington?" He nodded. I started to laugh; I couldn't help it. "And that's what you were afraid to tell me?" He nodded again, grinning in relief at my reaction. "When bigger jackasses are made, Sawyer, be sure you're standing in line. Wing Darlington could no more have—"

The telephone rang shrilly, and I moved automatically toward the hall to answer it. "Can I go now?" Sawyer asked from behind me.

"Sure," I said absently. "See you later." I hesitated before picking up the phone. What could Wing have been doing with George's car? It was an unlikely combination. But Wing Darlington kill George Pierson? They'd been best friends in school. It was ridiculous. Absurd. Totally—

The phone shrilled insistently, and I reached for it. "Yes?"

"I'm calling from a pay station, Jim." It was Veronica

150

Peters. I hadn't heard her voice in weeks. Her speech was slurred breathlessly, as if she'd been running. "I've just slipped out of Mr. Cartwright's office for a moment. They've brought that man over from Spartanburg to make a statement under a promise of immunity, Jim, and they're issuing a warrant for your arrest."

"Arrest? What the hell for? They've got a man's unsupported statement—" I didn't finish it. They had a man's unsupported statement about what he suspected had taken place, and no body. They'd never have a body.

Veronica was still talking. I heard what she was saying, but I couldn't concentrate on it. I was wishing I hadn't turned Graham Sawyer loose so soon. Wing Darlington? Wing had killed George Pierson? But that would mean— could mean—

"And Mr. Harrington called Frank Garvey and told him to get a group together to arrest you," Veronica concluded.

That roused me. "Group? What do you mean, a group?" I thought of something else. "Listen, they let you walk right out of the office to make this phone call to me?"

"I don't know, Jim. No one tried to stop me when I said I had to step out of the office for a minute."

I didn't like it. Were Harrington and his people so cocksure that they didn't care if she called me? Of course, they could be counting on the fact that we'd stopped seeing each other. Considering our parting, it was surprising she'd bothered to call. "Thanks for phoning, Veronica. I'll get this straightened out. You get back to the office before they miss you."

"You'll be careful, Jim?"

"Careful?" I knew I wasn't keeping the irritation out of my voice, but I couldn't help it. "What is there to be careful about? It doesn't amount to a thing. I appreciate your calling, though," I added hastily. "*You* be careful, and I'll be in touch. Good-bye now." I hung up while she was still trying to say something.

I stood there staring down at the phone. I knew I should be thinking about moving in on Harrington in a way that would cut his water off permanently. Sending

Frank Garvey to arrest me—what kind of cards did he think he was playing? They had nothing at all they could make stick.

But I couldn't focus on Harrington. Wing Darlington kept crowding him out of my mind: laughing, rough-housing, whoring, debonair, devil-may-care Wing. If Wing Darlington had killed George Pierson, what did it *mean*? I beat my brain around trying to find an answer and came up with nothing.

I left the phone and walked rapidly to the front door. The sight of Lud's car in the driveway slowed me; I'd forgotten that she had the station wagon. Well, this wouldn't wait. I'd take her car. I had trouble getting it started. Even after it caught, the motor banged and bucked on half its cylinders. Whoever washed it had sloshed water under the hood, I thought. I eased out of the driveway and headed for Wing's place.

The car jerked along, pooping and farting. I kept expecting it to dry out, but it didn't. It got worse. I pulled over to the curb under a streetlight, and got out and raised the hood. In the half-darkness, I felt around the spark plugs. They seemed dry, and the engine was definitely getting gas; it was just misfiring consistently. I removed a plug and tried to measure the spark gap by eye. It looked a bit wide. I gave it an experimental squeeze between thumb and forefinger and replaced it. There was no noticeable improvement. I got back into the car anyway and started off again. It backjumped every little bit, but it ran.

Wing's place was dark when I reached it, and I pulled into the curb and sat staring at it. My headache had reached boiler plate-factory proportions. I couldn't make up my mind whether I thought there was even a slight chance that Wing had killed George. *Could* he have done it? That was easier; if he ever decided to do it, he had nerve and to spare for the job. But *why*? I definitely wanted to talk to him. Where could I find him at this hour on a Friday night? The answer to that came as automatically as the response about his nerve: I'd find him at the cabin.

Since the car was so hard to start, I'd kept the motor running. As I started off again, a police cruiser passed me going the other way. It was probably my state of mental upset, but I thought the uniformed patrolman driving it turned for a quick look. It reminded me that I wanted no interruptions until I'd talked to Wing. I skirted the center of town and got out on the highway. With the motor wide open, the car ran better. Not good, but better. There was a serious loss of power, and at any other time I'd have done something about it at once.

It took me twenty-five minutes to reach the cabin. I couldn't see lights anywhere as I drove in, but I cut the engine and coasted the final seventy yards. I was glad I did because Wing's Galaxie was parked in the slot. I braked to a stop before I got close enough for the noise of the car's wheels on the gravel to be heard. That close, I could see a chink of light at a drawn side curtain. I got out of Lud's car and circled it to stay off the gravel, then walked on a soft cushion of pine needles. My route brought me almost to the rear of the cabin. Then I saw the silhouette of another car parked there. Its familiar outline brought me up short. Still not really believing it, I went over and put my hand on my own station wagon.

I turned and looked at the silent cabin. I started around it to the front, then walked back and reached through the station wagon's open front window and took from the glove compartment the Smith & Wesson .38 I'd carried there ever since the night I'd run into Whit Bailey in front of Veronica's apartment. I approached the front of the cabin noiselessly, dropped the gun in my jacket pocket, and took out my key. There wasn't a whisper of sound from inside. I inserted the key into the lock and turned it a hair at a time. There was the faintest of clicks; then the door opened. I waited another moment before widening the aperture sufficiently for me to slip inside.

They were in the large bedroom, and Lud was speaking. "—changes made," she was saying. "Sooner than you think."

"You're makin' heap powerful talk all of a sudden," I heard Wing's drawl. "For a gal who's been walkin' the chalk line you have lately. You still goin' to lie to me that Jim don't have nothin' on you?"

"I'll change the story slightly." Lud sounded pleased with herself. "What he had, he no longer has. And since he's unmanageable, and I no longer have need for him, he's at the end of the line. That's why I've kept Harrington on the sidelines. I can use him until we get your rough edges knocked off and I can present you to society and we can get married."

"You got me with that marriage bit once, sexy," Wing said. "You don't git me with it again."

"The hardest thing I've had to do was keep Tom from using this Manton until I was ready to have Tom pull the trigger," Lud continued. "When I get rid of Jim, the people who matter will go along with Harrington because there'll be no one else available. And I'll control him."

"Lord, you're mouthy tonight, woman," Wing said lazily. "Who's this Manton you're yammerin' about? An' get rid of ol' Jim? You could break all your pearly little teeth on *that* project, now you better believe it."

"I'm rid of him, Wing."

His voice altered as if he had changed position to look at her. "You're *rid* of him? What the hell you talkin' about?"

"He'll be picked up tonight on an investigation-of-murder charge and killed while resisting arrest."

"He'll be—*what*?" The bed creaked, and I heard the splat of Wing's bare feet hitting the floor. I moved silently toward the bedroom. "Now lissen here, Lud, have you gone crazy altogether?"

She laughed. "I'll tell you how sane I am. I've left him with a car that doesn't run properly so there's no chance of his outrunning a cruiser. If he should get to the car, which I doubt." Her tone changed. "Where do you think you're going?"

"To Jim, to straighten out this infernal mess you've cooked up. You must be out of your damn mind."

"Take your hand off those clothes!" Her voice had an edge like a factory whistle. "Unless you'd like to end up trying to answer some unanswerable questions about

154

George's death." Her voice changed again. "What are you upset about? You should be thanking me. You're his heir, you know, although I imagine I'll be entitled to a widow's third."

"Why, goddam you, Lud, he's my *partner*! I'll—"

"Hi, kids," I said from the doorway. Wing whirled from his standing position beside the bed; he hadn't a stitch on. Lud, on the bed, was wearing the same. It was like seeing the same movie twice. "Happy to see you making it with all my wives," I said to Wing. "It must save you a lot of time you'd otherwise spend chasing less available whores."

Lud spoke before Wing could. "What kick do you think you have coming?" she demanded. There was no fear in her voice. "You wouldn't touch me."

"There's that," I agreed. "But what about the interesting little conversation I just tuned in on?"

She was silent. I put my hand in my jacket pocket, and she started to get up. I took out the Smith & Wesson, and she shrank back upon the bed. Wing was watching me like a kingfisher over a pool. "I can understand your having me x'd out from the start, Lud," I said conversationally. "Considering the circumstances. But how do you think you're going to beat the angle of the movie film?"

"Put that gun away," she ordered. "You're not scaring anyone with it." Her eyes said differently, though.

"Let's hear how cleverly you outmaneuvered me on the film deal," I suggested. "And I'd recommend that you talk fast. You might run out of breath."

She wet her lips. "After I'd exhausted all other possibilities, I sent Andy Martin to every bank in this end of the state with a sample of your handwriting, looking for a safe deposit box in an assumed name." She was gathering confidence from the sound of her own voice. "When he finally located Mr. Joseph Winters' box over in Palmetto, I brought a man down from New York City to pose as an Internal Revenue field agent for those hick bank officials over there." She stopped.

"And the film is no longer in the box?"

155

"That's right," she said defiantly. "I burned it."

"So it comes down to this." I waved the gun at her.

"You're not going to use it."

I couldn't make up my mind. I couldn't kill her and salvage anything from the operation. But I couldn't do anything else, either. She'd boxed me in neatly from every point of the compass. She'd taken every single bit of initiative right out of my hands.

My frustration got through to her and inexplicably bolstered her confidence. "Look at the big man," she said to Wing. "Look at the giant intellect turning over." She turned to me. "I gave you every chance. *Every* chance. Didn't I?" She turned back to the silently watching Wing. "Look at him. Just look at his expression." It could have been hysteria, but she started to laugh. "He's—been planning for years—and now—he's run out of plans!" she got out between choking bursts of merriment.

A bright red flare went off inside my skull. "No!" she gasped as I walked to the bed. "NO!" She screamed it that time while trying to scramble off the bed. The gun went off by itself, five times. It polka-dotted her from her Adam's apple to her navel, knocking her onto her back. Her mouth opened as wide as her staring eyes; she made one deep whistling sound, and then her mouth went slack.

Wing hit me from my blind side like a runaway truck. The gun popped out of my hand into the air, and we both lunged for it. He caught it before it hit the floor. "My name ain't Bailey, hoss," he said softly.

I went after him, and he popped me on the side of the head with the gun. The room grew dark as I staggered up against a wall. I was just peeling myself off it to go after him again when we both heard it at the same time: sirens in the distance.

"Knock it off on the muscles," he ordered. He looked from me to Lud on the bed and back again. "Well, man, you just bought *all* the action," he continued bitterly. "Not even in this county do they issue licenses to kill *two* wives. Your ass has had the course, son."

"You sonofabitch, Wing—"

"Aaahhh, set it to music, hoss," he said wearily. "She did it to us both. 'Kill George for me, Wing, dear, an' we'll be married.'" He grinned mirthlessly. "So I was gonna show you who was goin' to be the real big shot around town." He gestured with the gun at the bed. "I been pluggin' that twice a week reg'lar since high school, but what the hell could I say to you the night out here you told me you were gonna marry her? We were partners, for God's sake! How do you think I felt? An' where did it leave me to go? After gettin' rid of George for her, she had me in her pocket."

I could see it all. Now that it was far too late, I could see every shade and nuance of Lud's skillful scheming.

The sirens were getting louder. I looked once more at her body, sprawled on the bed. "Get out of here, Wing," I said. "Cut out through the woods. They haven't got anything on you. She's the only other one who knows about George, and she's dead."

He shook his head. "They'd fetch it up soon's they started nosin' around. It makes too pretty a package for them to miss." He cocked an ear in the direction of the sirens. "You reckon that's the war party comin' after you?"

"I passed a cruiser on the way out here," I remembered. "He could have followed me."

"You goin' peaceable?" Wing asked me. He sounded honestly curious.

I thought about it for a minute. "I think not."

"So we play the hand," he said briskly. Naked, he walked to the gun rack and took down the deer rifle. "Better reload that thing," he said, tossing me the Smith & Wesson. Then he went around and turned off all the lights.

I went to the cabinet and reloaded the .38, then picked up a Colt Ace automatic and stuck it in my belt. "You could still make it into the woods," I was saying when a blinding sheet of light illuminated the interior of the cabin. A bullhorn blared shatteringly.

"Come on out of there, Wilson!" it blatted. "We know you're in there! Come out with your hands in the air!"

157

"You take this room an' I'll take the other," Wing said quickly. "Keep 'em amused longer that way." He strode to the window in the smaller bedroom across the hall, smashed the glass with the butt of the deer rifle, reversed the rifle while he was leaning out, and took out the spotlight with one shot. It went out in sections, and the room gradually darkened again. Wing pivoted quickly and fired to his right. "Someone slitherin' around out there," he explained. "See anything?"

"Nothing."

A ragged volley of shots ripped through the cabin, and a bullet pinged off a pipe. I knocked out the glass in the window in front of me, and when the crash died out, a voice drifted in to me clearly. "What're the *two* Wilson cars doin' out here?" it complained.

"Never mind," another voice said harshly. "Get out'n my way an' give me workin' room."

There was a staccato brrrtt-t-t-t-t, and a beehive of bullets went through the wall over my head. I heard the sound of Wing hitting the floor across the hall before I hit it myself. Plaster showered down from the wall in a fine spray. "Short party tonight, hoss," Wing called across to me. "That's Garvey. He's chopper-happy."

I fired quickly at moving shadows outside my window —whether men or not I couldn't be sure. "Move out into the hall, Wing," I said as softly as I could. Revolvers were popping all around us in the night. "That thing will take us out of here in one punch if we stay close to the walls."

Another spotlight came on and again illumined the cabin's interior. I could see Wing's grin as he inched his way out on his belly to join me. "Make me a reservation if you get there 'fore I do," he said as he fired through the front door. "For luck," he explained. "Shame not to get one or two of 'em first."

The machine gun started up again, this time on Wing's side of the cabin. His lips were still moving, but I couldn't hear what he was saying above the noise. Plaster spurted from the wall, baseboard-high. There was a loud *Spaaaang!* followed by a shrieking roar as a slug ricocheted from

158

the air conditioner. I heard Wing grunt, and I turned my head. He was limp on the floor. The battered slug had caught him in the forehead, laying it open an inch. I couldn't tell if it had killed him or not, but in another second it didn't make any difference because in his next pass, Garvey's creeping barrage laced into Wing's body from end to end. He jerked and twitched as the slugs bit into him, but there was no sign of life.

There was no future where I was. As soon as Garvey rounded the cabin again, I faced the same dose. If tear gas didn't arrive first. I got to my feet, picked up Wing's naked body, and cradled it in my left arm. Discarding the empty .38, I snatched the Colt from my belt. Something slapped my arm, which immediately began to burn. I ran into the other bedroom. A bullet in the fleshy part of the thigh almost brought me down, but I kept going. I went out through the window, jumping as high and as far as I could, still carrying Wing. If I could just make it to the pine trees—

I was still in the air when I saw Garvey rounding the corner of the cabin, his machine gun on his hip. I twisted to try to bring the Colt to bear on him, but my momentum was turning me the other way. He was good with his damn cornpopper; he picked me up with it in midair. For a second I felt the bullets ripping into Wing again, and then as I continued my helpless turning a sheet of flame ran down my back.

I never remembered hitting the ground.

The trial is almost over now. The verdict will be automatic, and so will the sentence.

I've attended the trial on a stretcher, since the machine gun bullets fused my spine, and I'm curious to know how they're going to manage getting me into the chair.

Nights, when there's time to think, I go back over the whole thing in my mind, wondering what I might have done differently that would have ensured a changed result. But it's history now.

I have only one worry left now, one fear.

If a softhearted politician should commute the sentence to life imprisonment, I don't know what I'd do.

Or perhaps I mean that I know all too well what I'd have to do.

Winner of the Edgar Allan Poe Award from the Mystery Writers of America, **Dan J. Marlowe**'s crime novels and short stories have been published in more than a dozen countries and languages, including Gallimard's *Série Noire* in France. Born in Lowell, Massachusetts, in 1914, Marlowe worked as a self-employed writer from 1957 until his death in Los Angeles in 1987.

BLACK LIZARD BOOKS

JIM THOMPSON
AFTER DARK, MY SWEET $3.95
THE ALCOHOLICS $3.95
THE CRIMINAL $3.95
CROPPER'S CABIN $3.95
THE GETAWAY $3.95
THE GRIFTERS $3.95
A HELL OF A WOMAN $3.95
NOTHING MORE THAN MURDER $3.95
POP. 1280 $3.95
RECOIL $3.95
SAVAGE NIGHT $3.95
A SWELL LOOKING BABE $3.95
WILD TOWN $3.95

HARRY WHITTINGTON
THE DEVIL WEARS WINGS $3.95
FIRES THAT DESTROY $4.95
FORGIVE ME, KILLER $3.95
A MOMENT TO PREY $4.95
A TICKET TO HELL $3.95
WEB OF MURDER $3.95

CHARLES WILLEFORD
THE BURNT ORANGE HERESY $3.95
COCKFIGHTER $3.95
PICK-UP $3.95

ROBERT EDMOND ALTER
CARNY KILL $3.95
SWAMP SISTER $3.95

W.L. HEATH
ILL WIND $3.95
VIOLENT SATURDAY $3.95

PAUL CAIN
FAST ONE $3.95
SEVEN SLAYERS $3.95

FREDRIC BROWN
HIS NAME WAS DEATH $3.95
THE FAR CRY $3.95

DAVID GOODIS
BLACK FRIDAY $3.95
CASSIDY'S GIRL $3.95
NIGHTFALL $3.95
SHOOT THE PIANO PLAYER $3.95
STREET OF NO RETURN $3.95

HELEN NIELSEN
DETOUR $4.95
SING ME A MURDER $4.95

DAN J. MARLOWE
THE NAME OF THE GAME IS DEATH $4.95
NEVER LIVE TWICE $4.95
STRONGARM $4.95
VENGEANCE MAN $4.95

MURRAY SINCLAIR
ONLY IN L.A. $4.95
TOUGH LUCK L.A. $4.95

JAMES M. CAIN
SINFUL WOMAN $4.95
JEALOUS WOMAN $4.95
THE ROOT OF HIS EVIL $4.95

PETER RABE
KILL THE BOSS GOODBYE $4.95
DIG MY GRAVE DEEP $4.95
THE OUT IS DEATH $4.95

HARDCOVER ORIGINALS:
LETHAL INJECTION by JIM NISBET $15.95
GOODBYE L.A. by MURRAY SINCLAIR $15.95

AND OTHERS...
FRANCIS CARCO • *PERVERSITY* $3.95
BARRY GIFFORD • *PORT TROPIQUE* $3.95
NJAMI SIMON • *COFFIN & CO.* $3.95
ERIC KIGHT (RICHARD HALLAS) • *YOU PLAY THE BLACK AND THE RED COMES UP* $3.95
GERTRUDE STEIN • *BLOOD ON THE DINING ROOM FLOOR* $6.95
KENT NELSON • *THE STRAIGHT MAN* $3.50
JIM NISBET • *THE DAMNED DON'T DIE* $3.95
STEVE FISHER • *I WAKE UP SCREAMING* $4.95
LIONEL WHITE • *THE KILLING* $4.95
JOHN LUTZ • *THE TRUTH OF THE MATTER* $4.95
ROGER SIMON • *DEAD MEET* $4.95
BILL PRONZINI • *MASQUES* $4.95
BILL PRONZINI & BARRY MALZBERG • *THE RUNNING OF BEASTS* $4.95
VICTORIA NICHOLS & SUSAN THOMPSON • *SILK STALKINGS* $16.95
THE BLACK LIZARD ANTHOLOGY OF CRIME FICTION
    Edited by EDWARD GORMAN $8.95
THE SECOND BLACK LIZARD ANTHOLOGY OF CRIME FICTION
    Edited by EDWARD GORMAN $15.95

Black Lizard Books are available at most bookstores or directly from the publisher. In addition to list price, please sent $1.00/postage for the first book and $.50 for each additional book to Black Lizard Books, 833 Bancroft Way, Berkeley, CA 94710. California residents please include sales tax.